# FLIGHT FROM BERLIN

# FLIGHT FROM BERLIN

## An SS Wotan Adventure

## Leo Kessler

5 2 4 3 1 0

# MORAY DISTRICT COUNCIL
# DEPARTMENT OF
# LEISURE AND LIBRARIES

This first world edition published in Great Britain 1995 by
SEVERN HOUSE PUBLISHERS LTD of
9–15 High Street, Sutton, Surrey SM1 1DF.
First published in the U.S.A. 1995 by
SEVERN HOUSE PUBLISHERS INC of
425 Park Avenue, New York, NY 10022.

British Library Cataloguing in Publication Data
Kessler, Leo
  Flight from Berlin
  I. Title
  823.914 [F]

  ISBN 0-7278-4730-9

Typeset by Hewer Text Composition Services, Edinburgh.
Printed and bound in Great Britain by
Hartnolls Ltd, Bodmin, Cornwall.

"What yer gonna do – let 'em purple shaft yer? No sir, frig 'em all."

*The Sayings of Sergeant Schulze*

# AUTHOR'S NOTE

In the last week of April 1945, Berlin, the capital of the Third Reich, was in its death throes. Virtually surrounded by the Red Army, it was defended by the scum of Europe. In the cellars of the bombed, shell-shattered houses, thousands of people sheltered, enjoying one last colossal orgy of sex and drink before the inevitable happened. Those who could had already fled. Those who couldn't knew that only one fate awaited them, especially if they were high-ranking officials in the Nazi Party – *DEATH!* If they didn't kill themselves, then the victorious Russians would.

In the end those sheltering in the *"Führerbunker"*, Hitler's own personal bunker underneath the ruins of the Reich Chancellery, the two remaining top Nazis, Hitler, and his Minister of Propaganda and Public Enlightenment, Dr Josef Goebbels, both shot themselves and had their bodies cremated.

But there was one prominent Nazi in that bunker, the most powerful man in Germany after Hitler, who did not want to die that last terrible week of April fifty years ago. His name was Martin Bormann. Officially he was Hitler's secretary, but in reality he ran the Nazi Party. Outside of Hitler's entourage he was virtually unknown. There were few photographs of him in existence – indeed when they came to try him in absentia at Nuremberg, the Allied authorities could not find a single photo of the surly-faced, heavy-chinned Bormann, who looked like a prizefighter gone to seed.

Over the years Bormann had methodically picked off his rivals – Hess, Himmler, Goering. "I hope he is frying in hell," Goering exclaimed after his own capture. Now this April, Bormann, using the same patient, methodical techniques, prepared to escape to a new life of power and influence in South America. When this sinister man of mystery left the Führerbunker for the last time on May 1st, 1945, a new mystery engulfed him. For nearly half a century after he ventured into the night in a Berlin which was dying under the Russian onslaught, the world's newspapers carried sensational reports of his whereabouts. He was spotted in Egypt, then in the Argentine. Others reported him living like a king in a strange neo-Nazi colony in the heart of the South American jungle . . .

In reality, Bormann had not survived for more than forty-eight hours after he had started his escape. Those who had known the truth about the fate of Martin Bormann were soon dead themselves or had good reasons for keeping their mouths shut. All save ex-Sergeant Schulze and ex-Corporal Matz, formerly of SS Assault Regiment Wotan. This is their tale, one of treachery, double-dealing, blackmail and murder. It is not a pleasant one, but then in those days, half a century ago, there weren't many pleasant tales.

L. K. 1994. Summer.

# PART ONE

## *Into the Trap*

"*Scheisse*, now we've really landed in the pisspot and they're going to do it to us."

*The Sayings of Sergeant Schulze*

# ONE

"Well, I'll go and crap in my cap!" Sergeant Schulze yelled above the thunder and roar of the Russian guns. "Cast yer frigging glassy orbs over there, Matzi!"

"Over where, you big stream o' piss?" Matzi yelled back. Corporal Matz, Schulze's long-time running mate in SS Assault Regiment Wotan was crouched with the rest of the reinforcements in the shelter of the ruined apartment house, its sides pocked with shell marks like the symptoms of some loathsome skin disease.

"Over there!" Schulze snorted, pointing with a finger that looked like a fat hairy sausage.

Matz nodded. He saw what the big, red-faced NCO meant. The Russian gunfire had hit what looked like a zoo. The shell-pitted open space was filled with dead animals of all kinds. There were slaughtered giraffes lying everywhere like felled multicoloured trees. There were blooded ostriches dead in a scattering of black and white feathers, their great legs and clawed feet crumpled like cables. Crouched in a shell hole a middle-aged woman with a red cross on her dirty apron and wearing a helmet that was too large for her was tying a bandage around the wounded arm of a monkey. Two elderly keepers, tears streaming down their faces, were bearing out a small dead brown bear on a stretcher.

"Great crap on the Christmas tree!" Matz exclaimed.

"Frigging pathetic, ain't it? I mean yer get used to seeing soldiers get the chop. But animals—" He shook his head sadly.

A zebra tottered past the sheltering men, dragging its bloody stump of a shattered limb. Grimly Schulze raised his machine pistol and pressed the trigger. A line of sudden red buttonholes appeared the length of the animal's black-and-white striped hide. It went down in a heap, twitched in convulsions for a few seconds and then lay still.

"You did right, Schulze," Matz said. "Poor shit—" The rest of his words were drowned by the roar of plane engines. The little Fiesler Storch observer planes which had brought them into the besieged capital were attempting to take off. Three abreast, they were racing down the battle-littered boulevard, going flat out. But already the Russians had spotted them. Machine-gun fire erupted from a line of houses some five hundred metres away and someone had alerted the enemy light flak. Shells zapped into the sky. In a lethal morse, streams of glowing white 20mm tracer streaked upwards.

A plane was struck. It shivered like a live thing attempting to ward off a blow. To no avail! The Storch's left wing fell off. It dropped out of the sky like a stone. It hit the cobbles. Next moment it exploded in a vivid ball of flame.

"Poor shit," one of the handful of Wotan men commented.

"Knock it off," Schulze snarled, as the other two planes rose higher and higher heading straight west and away from ruined Berlin. "They're going home to momma, a nice bowl of fart soup" – he meant pea soup – "and a bottle of suds and if they're lucky a bit o' the old two-backed beast. *We're* stuck in Berlin. But I'll tell you one thing, lads, and yer better pin this behind yer ears." He looked grimly round the circle of tough hard faces, for they were all veterans, the last of SS Wotan. "Mrs Schulze's handsome son ain't gonna die here in Berlin. Nor are you lot, shower of shit that you are, if I have my way. Whatever kind of Ascension Day mission" – he meant suicidal mission – "this frigging is, we're gonna get out of it." He raised his voice as the thunder of the Russian guns grew in intensity. "Have yer got that?"

"Yes, Sarge," they answered as one. They knew the big, red-faced Schulze. If anyone could get them out of the mess they seemed to have landed in, it would be Schulze. Already at the reinforcement centre where what remained of the shattered SS regiments had been quartered, he had tried to steal discharge papers for the lot of them from the adjutant's office. But before he could acquire the official stamp for the stolen documents, they had been ordered to take off for Berlin which was now completely surrounded by the Russians.

"I know yer full of piss an' vinegar, Schulze" – Matz expressed all their thoughts as the Russian guns rumbled and all around them what was left of German-held Berlin died – "but you'll do it, old house." He patted the big NCO affectionately.

"Get yer frigging paw off'n me!" Schulze snorted. "What d'yer think I am – a frigging warm brother?" He meant homosexual. He raised his right haunch and let rip one of his massive farts which were celebrated and well known throughout the SS NCO corps. "Now we're all gonna ride on that—" He stopped short, face suddenly set, hard and determined. "Hold on to yer hats, lads," he exclaimed. "Here comes the reception committee."

A Volkswagen jeep was racing past the zoo, followed by angry white and red tracer. Frantically the driver zig-zagged from side to side to put the Russians, dug-in in the shattered house to the right, off their aim.

"All right," Schulze snapped urgently. "Don't just stand there like a frigging spare penis at a wedding." He unslung his Schmeisser again. "Give the poor shits, whoever they are, covering fire. *Dalli . . . dalli!*"

Hastily the dozen or so Wotan men started firing, peppering the houses some two hundred metres away with their fire. Bullets whined off the walls. Brick erupted in angry white and red spurts. Windows shattered. But the enemy fire died away and moments later the driver of the Volkswagen braked with a howl of rubber, slewed the vehicle round and into the shelter of the wall where they crouched. Next moment, sobbing for breath as if he had just run a great race, the driver slumped over the wheel, helmeted head resting on his arms.

But his passenger was energetic enough. He sprang out of the back seat, Schmeisser bouncing up and down on his bemedalled chest, his one good hand resting on his pistol holster, as if he expected he might have to use it at any moment. "Who's the senior NCO here?" he demanded in an accent which Schulze couldn't quite identify.

Schulze stared at the officer. He was tall, erect and tough looking. He was a front swine and no rear echelon stallion, that was clear enough. His left arm was of wood and a black patch covered his left eye. The Silver Wound Medal on his chest indicated he had been wounded three times. Schulze clicked to attention. "Sergeant Schulze, and fifteen men of SS Assault Regiment Wotan, present and correct!" he bellowed as if he was back on the parade ground, and saluted.

The hard-faced officer touched his riding crop to his helmet, adorned with the black runic double "S" of the Armed SS, and snapped, "All right, this is the drill, and

6

I'm glad to have you Wotan men under my command. I've heard good things of you."

Yer haven't heard I'm about to cream my drawers with fright, Matz told himself but he kept that thought to himself. Behind him another apartment house was hit, its walls shaking like a theatre backdrop. Masonry started to crash to the ground.

"We're dug-in to the rear of the zoo," the strange officer continued. "But the Ivans" – he meant the Russians – "have damned well infiltrated between here and our positions. We've got to winkle them out in order to stabilize our positions at the zoo. *Klar?*"

"Clear," they answered as one, knowing that they were going straight into action.

"Good," the officer snapped. "All right, from now onwards you belong to Battle Group van de Brug." He tapped his chest with his cane. "That's me." He grinned suddenly to reveal a set of gleaming stainless steel teeth. "Play ball with me and you'll have all the gash and suds I can find for you." He lowered his voice dramatically and menacingly. "Do me down and I'll bite the balls off'n you with these metal choppers of mine. *Klar?*"

"*Klar!*" they answered as one once again.

"*Gut.*" He turned swiftly and addressed the young driver slumped over the wheel, his skinny shoulders heaving to and fro as if he were heartbroken. "Gaston," he barked. "*Ça suffit. Dans un minute, roulez, lentement.*"

The boy wiped the tears from his pale face and said thickly, "*Oui, mon captaine!*"

Schulze gasped. "Christ on a frigging crutch," he exclaimed. "A frog! What next? – A frigging frog in the SS. What are things frigging coming to?"

But Schulze was in for another surprise. Van de Brug

slapped his cane hard against his boot and snapped, "*Pedro, que haces, hombre?*"

A dark face peered over the back of the car and Schulze saw that there had been someone else in the back seat all the time. "*A su servicio, Senor Capitano,*" the swarthy SS man replied.

"Well, I'll go and piss in my boot," Matz gasped. "A *dago!*"

"By the Great Whore of Buxtehude," Schulze breathed, "what kind of outfit is this then – the frigging Foreign Legion?"

Van de Brug turned and grinned. "Yes, in a way it is. I'm Dutch you see. We are the last scrapings of the barrel. Dutchmen, Frenchmen, Spaniards – we've even got an American and two Tommies – and all of us are prepared to die for the Führer." He winked and Schulze didn't know whether to take him seriously or not. One thing he did know. These renegades were going to die in Berlin. They had no alternative. They couldn't go home now. But he and his men weren't. Of that, Sergeant Schulze was absolutely, totally certain.

With his good hand, van de Brug placed his whistle in his teeth and shrilled three blasts on it. It was the signal. Gaston crashed home the gear.

# TWO

The underground room stank of scent, sweat, schnapps – and sex. The teleprinter operator lay gasping over the desk, her skirt rolled up to reveal her white, plump bottom, her knickers furled around her thick sturdy ankles. Martin Bormann, the Führer's secretary, opened his breeches. His penis stood erect like a policeman's baton. He seized hold of her buttocks with his thick fingers and pulled the cheeks apart. With a grunt he thrust home his penis. She gasped – whether with delight or pain, he didn't know or care. All he cared about was his own pleasure. "You're going to enjoy this, Annemarie," he gasped thickly and thrust himself even deeper into that juicy wetness.

"Please, please, Herr Reichsleiter," the girl choked. "Please – *more!*"

He thrust even harder, pumping himself into the girl.

She started to wriggle and tremble, so that he had to hold hard to her buttocks to prevent her from slipping off the desk.

He increased his efforts, sweat breaking out on his fat angry face like that of a boxer gone to seed. His fat belly slapped against her buttocks. His penis went in and out with a soft sucking noise. She wriggled more and more. Strangled little meaningless cries were coming out from her wide gaping mouth. He could see the beads of sweat

9

trickling down the sides of her face. It was flushed an angry red. She was enjoying every second of it, he told himself. "Come on, bitch!" he cried through gritted teeth as if he were angry with her. "*Come . . . come!*"

In the same moment that his spine arched like a taut bow, she cried out loud and suddenly went limp in his hands. Next instant he ejaculated and a great Russian shell slammed into the side of the upper bunker making it tremble and shake like a live thing. "*Gross Gott!*" he cursed, as he lolled over her wet naked body, all passion spent. "Why in the name of three devils can't they leave us in peace – just for a while?" he moaned.

She wriggled out from beneath him and pulled up her knickers. She ran her hand down his face lovingly, hair matted and sweat soaked. "Poor *Reichsleiter*," she breathed. "You have so many cares."

Roughly he pushed her hand away. There were fifty women in the Führer's typing-and-teleprinter pool which was under his command and he had had one of them for every day they had been in the bunker. Tomorrow he would pleasure yet another of them. He didn't need Annemarie any more. "You may go now," he ordered, buttoning up his flies. "I must see if the Führer has any wishes before he turns in for the night."

Like a schoolgirl she curtseyed and said, "Thank you, *Reichsleiter*, you are very kind to me." She slipped her frock over her head and went out.

Bormann frowned. Now, although they were deep underground in the gardens of the shattered chancellery, he could still hear the dull roar of the Soviet artillery. Once again he told himself that they were almost surrounded and that apart from the sizeable German force holding the zoo area there would soon be no way out of a doomed Berlin. He looked at himself in the mirror on the wall, checking if his tie was straight and his tunic was in order before he went up to the Führer's apartment. "I don't want to die," he said to the mirror. "I'm too young to die. There are so many women still to be conquered. There are other things too . . ." He broke off, tears welling up in his eyes in self-pity. He rubbed his knuckles into them and wiped away the tears. "Be brave," he urged himself. "There are ways and means. Martin, you won't go down with the sinking ship. *Los!*"

Confidently Bormann set off on his way through the bunker, which had been built twenty metres below the chancellery two years before, heading for the part occupied by the Führer. The *Führerbunker*, as it was called, consisted of eighteen rooms, all of them small, cramped and uncomfortable. SS men and officials sat or slumped against the walls everywhere as he strode down the corridor and Bormann noted to his annoyance that they didn't snap to attention on seeing him as they had done only the week before. Indeed some of them didn't even bother to take the cigarettes out of their mouth when he passed. Others, too, he saw had been drinking. He shook his head. Morale in the bunker was collapsing rapidly, he told himself.

He passed the shaft which led up to the observation tower and the entrance to the six rooms which Hitler occupied with his mistress, Eva Braun, a woman, he knew, who hated him. Not that that mattered, he thought. Hitler relied upon him totally. Whatever that Bavarian cow and slut said about his womanizing would have no effect on Hitler. The Führer took no notice of her utterances. After all, she was just a piece of gash who spread her legs obediently, whenever the Führer felt so inclined, which was not often he guessed. He smirked and his hand fell to his flies. Now, with what he had in his breeches, he'd

11

really make Eva Braun's eyes pop. The thought cheered him up mightily and when he entered the conference room at the end of the corridor, he was actually smiling.

Field Marshal Keitel, tall, stiff and wooden, was briefing Hitler on the military situation for the last time that April day, as a smiling Bormann entered. "*Mein Führer*," he was pontificating in that lordly manner of his, "it is clear that the Russian ring around Berlin will close in a few days, perhaps even hours. There is still an escape route to the south to the mountains around Obersalzburg. That's where all the Reich's ministries are going and we have a sizeable force of good troops down there." Keitel stared hard at Hitler, who was sipping peppermint tea and occasionally stroking his favourite Alsatian bitch, Blondi. "*Mein Führer*, a decision has to be made – *soon.*"

Bormann's smile vanished. He tensed. This was the moment he had been waiting for ever since they had moved underground from the ruined Reich Chancellery above. Once out of this damned bunker and far away in the Austrian mountains there were all sorts of ways to survive. But to stay in the Berlin bunker until the Russians stormed it – Bormann shuddered involuntarily. It was a thought he dreaded to think out to the end.

Hitler paused with his cup at his lips, held in a hand that trembled violently. "I do not feel I can make that decision just yet," he said slowly and carefully, as if he were considering the matter deeply. "The time has not yet come for drastic and overwhelming decisions of that nature."

Bormann's face fell.

"Five minutes ago," Hitler continued, "I just received word that our *Luftwaffe* was able to ferry in by air a contingent of the famous SS Assault Regiment Wotan." He smiled weakly at Keitel and the other officers present.

"I realize that they could not get in a large number of soldiers, but as long as we can move in troops, especially of the quality of the Wotan men, then I feel we have no reason to flee Berlin . . ." He stopped short.

Heinz Linge, his immensely tall servant, was standing at the door, looking very worried and holding a piece of paper in his hand.

"What is it, Linge?" Hitler asked a little impatiently. He hated to be disturbed when he was talking, which was most of the time.

"This has been just sent over from the news agency, *mein Führer*," Linge answered in that grave sombre voice of his. "I thought it so important that I ventured to disturb you."

"*Schon gut*," Hitler said. "Give it to me." He took the message and with a trembling hand placed his nickel-rimmed glasses on his nose. Then he began to read it aloud. "According to information sent to Anthony Eden, British Foreign Minister in San Francisco, a message from Himmler guaranteeing German unconditional surrender, but not to Russia, has been conveyed to British and US Governments . . ." Hitler broke off reading, his sallow sunken face suddenly flushing a deep crimson with rage. "Where did this message come from, Linge?" he demanded. "Where did the news agency get it?"

Linge licked suddenly dry lips. He knew the signs. Hitler was about to go into one of his tantrums. "From a broadcast of the BBC, *mein Führer*," he answered.

Wildly Hitler read on, his whole body beginning to tremble with rage. "Himmler is authoritatively stated to have informed Western Allies he is in position to arrange surrender and he himself is in favour of the same." Wildly Hitler threw the paper at the floor. "Vile traitor!" he snorted, spittle flying from his slack lips. "My own loyal

13

Himmler, the head of my SS, has now betrayed me. Am I surrounded by such traitors? What is Goering up to as well? Is he already talking to the enemy, eh?"

Bormann was only half listening to the Führer's ranting. His mind was racing electrically as he realised that this must be the last straw for Hitler. If Himmler, his loyal follower for so many years, right since the beginning of the Movement back in the '20s, was betraying him behind his back, he knew that Hitler would realise that there was no hope. Would the treachery signal the end for him? If so, what was he, Bormann, going to do? How was he to save himself if the Führer decided, as he thought he would, to stay in Berlin?

"*Mein Führer.*"

Bormann was startled. It was Keitel, who he had always thought of as a lackey, actually breaking into the Führer's tirade against Himmler.

"*Ja, Keitel?*"

"We must forget Himmler, *mein Führer*. I must inform you that we will be out of food and ammunition within two days. Then the troops defending Berlin will no longer have any means of resisting. As a soldier I suggest we make a breakout immediately." Before Hitler had time to object, Keitel launched into the details of his plan.

Hitler listened moodily, while again Bormann waited tensely. "What if the breakout succeeded Keitel? If we did manage to escape to the Austrian Alps, we'd be walking into another trap – an area surrounded by the enemy in Italy and Southern Germany." He shrugged and Bormann's heart sank. "Am I, the Führer, supposed to sleep in an open field or in a farmhouse or something like that and just wait for the end? *No*, it would be far better for me to remain in the Chancellery." Wearily, he rose to his feet and the officers present clicked to attention.

"I shall now go to my private apartments, *meine Herren.
Gute Nacht.*"

"*Gute Nacht, mein Führer,*" they answered dutifully,
as Hitler tottered out dragging his damaged left leg
behind him.

Bormann waited till he had gone before crossing to
Keitel to ask, "Well, Keitel, what do you think?"
Keitel looked down at the pudgy Party official super-
ciliously, not attempting to conceal his contempt. The
National Socialist Party was finished now and with it
Reichsleiter Bormann. He, Keitel, no longer needed to
be afraid of the man who had once been the power
behind Hitler's throne. "What do *I* think?" he asked
coldly, as if making up for all the years that he had
been ignored by Bormann. "Since you ask, however, I
shall tell you. The Führer will end his life here. It might be
tonight, tomorrow," he shrugged carelessly, "perhaps the
day after tomorrow. But once the food and ammunition
run out and the soldiers up there start surrendering, that
will have to be the time. He knows that if the Russians
ever take him alive, they'll put him a cage and display him
in the streets of Moscow – as they do with their bears."
He laughed grimly.

Bormann repressed his anger, clenching his fists to keep
his temper under control. How dare this toy soldier talk
to him, the second most powerful man in the Reich, like
this? "What will you do?" he asked, fighting to keep his
voice calm.

"The obvious. I don't want to die in this golden cage
– even for the Führer. I'm leaving this very night – and
remember this, Bormann. If you stay you've got exactly
forty-eight hours, at the most, to live." Keitel grinned
maliciously and then without another word, he turned and
strode away, pushing his way through the red-faced young

officers and secretaries who were now getting drunk. With the Führer in bed, they were letting their hair down. By midnight they'd be indulging in the usual nightly sex orgy; their drunken dance of death.

Bormann watched Keitel go, his face a mixture of hate and envy. He wished he could accompany him but he daren't leave the Bunker until the Führer was dead.

One of the drunken secretaries had taken off her frock and was now dancing on top of the table in her black underwear and silk stockings, cheered on by the excited young officers. But Bormann, whose sex drive was almost insatiable, had no eyes for the voluptuous blonde secretary. Slowly he walked back to his own room next to the dynamo which supplied the bunker with power, not even noticing the stink that came from the place this night; his mind was too full.

*He had to have a plan. Dammit, he had to have a plan of escape . . .*

# THREE

"All right, you perverted banana-suckers," Schulze yelled above the angry snap-and-crackle of the Russian small arms fire. "Get in among those Ivans. *Los*. Now come on, you jam-shitting stubble hoppers – *move it!*"

The Wotan men needed no urging. As Gaston slewed to a halt and dived out of the side of the Volkswagen, they rushed the houses, firing from the hip as they ran. A Russian loomed up from a ditch. He was a big man, an evil grin on his pockmarked face, as he raised his tommy gun prior to letting Schulze have a burst. But the big Wotan NCO was quicker off the mark. "Try this on for frigging size!" he cried happily and whipped a stick grenade out of his boot. In one and the same movement, he lobbed the bomb at the foxhole and ducked. A crash, a shriek, a burst of flame and the Russian's helmeted head, like a child's abandoned football, came rolling to a stop where he crouched.

Van de Brug yelled his approval and, twisting from left to right, raked the upper windows of the houses with his Schmeisser. A man screamed and fell out of one of them like a sack of wet cement. They rushed on, carried away by the wild unreasoning bloodlust of war.

Matz belted his wooden foot against the nearest door. It flew open. A Russian crouched there against the wall, tommy gun raised. Matz beat him to it. Wizened face set

17

and hard, he fired from the hip. The Russian screamed shrilly. His hands clawed the air, as if he were climbing the rungs of an invisible ladder. Next moment he pitched face forward to the ground, dead before he hit the floor. Matz pushed by him. Suddenly he spotted the flask at the Russian's hip. He bent down, pulled out the cork and smelled it. *"Vodka!"* he yelled exuberantly in the same instant that Schulze came running, great chest heaving frantically, through the door. "Did . . . I hear . . . someone mention . . . vodka?" he choked.

Matz didn't answer. He couldn't. He was already crouched next to the dead body, taking great swigs of the fiery spirits.

Schulze gave him a friendly clout about the ears which almost knocked him off his feet. "Hey, apeturd," he exclaimed, "what yer got friends for if yer can't share a little suds with 'em?"

"Go and fart in the wind," Matz said scornfully, forcing himself to take his mouth away from the flask like a reluctant baby being refused its mother's breast. "When it comes to firewater I ain't got no friends so . . ." He stopped short. Above the snap-and-crackle of the fire fight taking place in and around the houses, he could hear another sound, an ominous, frightening one, the clatter of tank tracks. "Get a load of that, Schulze," he said hastily.

Schulze forgot the vodka. He cocked his head to one side. "T-34s, Russki T-34s, by the sound of it," he concluded.

Matz nodded his head grimly.

"That's really put the clock in the pisspot," Schulze snapped. "Come on, you little streak of wet piss, let's go and have a look-see."

Together they doubled to the rear of the house. A

skinny runt of a Russian soldier came out of a side door, an axe in his hand. Schulze hardly seemed to hesitate. He raised his heavy, cruelly shod jackboot and kicked the runt in the crotch. The Russian dropped the axe. He screamed, his false teeth bulging foolishly out of his gaping mouth. He went down vomiting and holding his ruined crotch as he writhed from side to side. "Wonder if he was going to chop a bit o' firewood?" Schulze said pleasantly, as they came out into the open.

Red signal flares were shooting into the sky everywhere, indicating that the hard-pressed Russian defenders of the houses were asking for help. That explained the presence of two T-34 tanks, labouring their way up the incline which led to the back of the line of houses, great long 75mm guns swinging from side to side like the snouts of primeval monsters seeking out their prey.

Schulze pulled a face. "Sod this for a game o' cards," he snorted. "We've got nothing we can use against them."

"Well," Matz concluded, "we've got to find something, or them moveable tin boxes are going to make mincemeat out of us."

"Yes, you're right," Schulze agreed, a note of urgency in his voice now. "As soon as we've cleared these houses, they'll come for us. We've got to do for the Ivans before then. But how?"

"See that shell hole at three o'clock. About hundred and fifty metres away from here," Matz said.

"Got it. But what about it?"

"It's right in the path of the Ivans. If we can get in there, let 'em roll over us . . ."

"You mean, *tackle them from the rear?*"

"Yes." Matz answered simply.

Schulze gulped at the thought of letting a forty-ton Russian tank roll over him. It was something that could frighten the bravest of men. But he knew it was the only way. "Grenades?"

"Yes. Down the turret hatch. That'll give 'em a nasty headache." Matz laughed though he had never felt less like laughing. "You'd better tackle the first one. With my pegleg, I'm a bit slow." He slapped his wooden leg, as if to emphasize the point. "I'll do the second Ivan."

Schulze nodded his understanding. "All right, then," he said, his voice a little shaky as he thought of what was soon to come, "let's get on with the frigging nasty business."

Together, crouched low, making the smallest possible target, they hurried through the smoke of battle to the big shell hole. There were two dead Russians sprawled out in the extravagant postures of those who had been done violently to death in a hole. That didn't worry the two running mates. They had seen enough dead Russians in their time. Schulze pushed them to one side, saying in an exaggerated accent, "Excuse me, gentlemen, but we need the room. We have an important appointment in a moment." Then his grin vanished and he concentrated on the task ahead. One slip, he knew, and those churning tracks would turn the attacker into a bloody mess. "I'll recommend you, Matzi, for a second close combat badge if we pull it off," he yelled above the roar of the tanks' engines.

"Frig that for a tale," Matz yelled back, his face just as set and tense as the two Russian tanks got closer and closer. "Recommend me for a nice safe job in an old soldiers' home, complete with plenty of beaver and as much firewater as I can drink . . ." Then he fell silent. The tanks were almost upon them now.

They crouched there, huddled into a tense ball, hearts pounding frantically, nerves racing with electric swiftness. The roar got closer and closer. The clanking and rattling drowned out every other sound. "*Here they come!*" Schulze shrieked.

They tensed. The first monster was above them. The din was awesome. Their ears threatened to burst at any moment. Their nostrils were assailed by the cloying, nauseating stink of oil. They cowered there, trembling all over, feeling the hot oil drip on their hunched shoulders, as the churning roaring tracks, only centimetres away from their frail bodies, began to cross the hole. Abruptly their world was a black, howling, frightening pit. It seemed never ending. Schulze wanted to scream with fear. He caught himself just in time. He felt the air sucked cruelly from his lungs. His great chest started to heave. He was choking. He couldn't stand this much longer. He gasped and choked. Would the horror never end? He'd throw himself under the nearest track and have done with it. Let the steel monster have its way with him. Only let it end . . .

Then it was gone, leaving behind it the stench of fuel oil. Schulze braced himself and then he levered himself out of the pit, "*I'm off Matzi!*" Groggily he started after the first T-34, stumbling through the churned up earth. Ahead of him he could see the dull red glow of the twin exhausts through the wall of flying pebbles and earth.

Behind him the other T-34 cleared the pit, leaving Matz to clamber out behind it and commence his stalking. As he stumbled forward Matz told himself that he hoped the first tank's wave of earth and stones would cover Schulze long enough for him to get aboard the first tank. If the gunner of the second one spotted the big noncom – Matz decided it wasn't right to think that particular dreadful thought through to its conclusion.

Schulze summoned up the last of his strength. He grabbed hold of the back of the tank and swung himself aboard. He poised on the metal deck unsteadily, grenade whipped out of his boot, peering towards the turret. The gunner or tank commander hadn't closed the hatch. It was ideal for him. He stole forward, balancing himself as best he could. Suddenly there was the soft whirr of electricity. The gun came swinging round with the turret. Down below the crew must have heard him.

The long, overhanging cannon missed him by millimetres. It was so close that he could feel the heat from its muzzle. He knew he had no time to lose. In a second they'd close the hatch. Hastily he pulled the china pin at the base of the stick grenade. He lobbed it up and right into the turret. Next moment he dived over the side, just as the gunner of the second tank spotted him and let loose a vicious burst of machine-gun fire. Tracer whizzed all about him as he fell to the ground in the churned-up earth and buried his head in it.

There was a thick, muffled crump. A mushroom of black smoke erupted from the open turret. The T-34's right track snapped. It rolled out behind the tank like a severed limb. Someone screamed shrilly. A man in a tanker's leather helmet flung himself over the hatch. He was already on fire. Desperately he dived for the ground, but Schulze didn't give him a chance. As he lay there he fired a rapid burst in the same instant that the gunner of the second tank opened fire, too, peppering the ground all about the big NCO with slugs. Not for long.

A moment later Matz's grenade exploded as he flung himself over the side of the doomed T-34. It reared up in the air like a wild horse being put to the saddle for the first time. Next instant it exploded in a massive burst of angry flame, with ammunition zig-zagging crazily all over the place. No one escaped.

Suddenly there was a loud echoing silence, as the two

friends and comrades, separated from each other by a hundred metres, stared at each other, dazed and a little bewildered. "Well, I'll go and shit green apples," Schulze said slowly. "We've done it, old house . . . we've done it!"

"Dicing with death," Matz answered, his teeth very white against his smoke-blackened face. "Dicing with frigging death, as always." Slowly, almost suddenly, he rose to his feet. "Come on, Schulze, let's go and find the others." Without looking back to see if his old running mate was following, he started to limp back to the houses, shoulders hunched like those of a man who bore a very heavy weight. Behind him the two tanks continued to burn furiously, charring and shrinking the dead man to the size of a pygmy.

# FOUR

Dawn!

The camp of the Battle Group van de Brug was set in the forest, and it was still hushed in sleep although the Russian batteries surrounding Berlin were already firing once more. Over the centre of the beleaguered city new fires were beginning to burn.

Slowly the tired veterans of Wotan filed through the camp, a collection of small, camouflaged tents, each one dug into a hole for protection. Schulze wrinkled his nose as they did so. The whole place stank of unwashed bodies, stale urine and defeat. A sentry moved by, his rifle slung carelessly, hands in his pocket, a cigarette dangling from the corner of his mouth. He saw van de Brug but didn't salute.

"He looks like some sort of yellow Chink," Matz commented, as the sloppy sentry disappeared into the pines.

"He's a Turcoman," van de Brug informed Matz. "This is today's elite Armed SS" – van de Brug emphasized the words cynically – "recruited from a dozen European and Asian countries, including such *honorary* Aryans as Siberians, Tartars and that Turcoman over there. And of course we have real Aryans in the shape of our *Ami* friend and the two Tommies. Why you and the others of the Wotan are the only Germans in Battle Group van de Brug."

"But what in three devils' name," Schulze snorted, "makes these men volunteer to join the *Waffen SS* at this stage of the war when everybody knows that Germany is up to its hooter in crap?" Schulze looked bewildered.

Van de Brug laughed drily. "Never fear, dear Sergeant Schulze, I'm no idiot, I've seen the writing on the wall, too, but you know what they say in German – *mitgegangen, mit gefangen, mitgehangen\**. There's no way back for me and there's no way back for them as well." His face hardened. "We'll all die in Berlin."

Schulze looked hard at the Dutchman, but this time, he could see, the Captain was no longer cynical. He meant every word he said. They were all renegades. There was no alternative for them but to fight and die for a nation to which they didn't belong. "But not us, old friend," a hard little voice at the back of Schulze's head rasped. "We're not going to die for the frigging One Thousand Year Reich. *We're going to survive!*"

"Ah, there's Sturmbannführer Kuehn," van de Brug exclaimed, as they neared the centre of the camp in the woods. He indicated a tall, smartly dressed officer striding purposefully towards them, Schmeisser hung over his shoulder, stick grenades in both boots. "Our American friend."

He stopped the regulation six paces in front of van de Brug, clicked to attention and snapped in almost accentless German, "*Sturmbannführer Kuehn meldet sich zur Stelle!*" He saluted.

With a pleased smile, van de Brug returned the very smart salute, while Schulze weighed up the foreign officer, who, though van de Brug had said was American, obviously was of German parentage to judge by his accent.

---

\* Roughly – "went with, caught with, hanged with".

25

Kuehn looked sharp. He had keen blue eyes set in a tough, cynical brown face which gave away little. His features radiated strength, however, inner knowledge and power. He was an officer, Schulze told himself, he wouldn't like to cross.

"Kuehn," van de Brug said, "this is Sergeant Schulze and what is left of SS Assault Regiment Wotan. You've heard of it?"

"Yessir. I've heard of it." Kuehn looked up at Schulze, seemingly summed him up in a glance, then looked at the other veterans, all of them dirty and unshaven and hung with weapons. He nodded his head, as if in approval.

"All right, Kuehn. They're in your charge now. Get them fed and washed. I don't think we'll have much time to hang around this day." He nodded in the direction of the centre of the city, with the distress rockets hissing into the dawn sky, summoning help. "We'll be facing – er shot, shell and shit before the day's end, that's for certain. I'm off to get washed and swallow a glass of gunfire." He meant a glass of fiery rum and water. He grinned. "Rank hath its privileges. *Weitermachen*."

Kuehn and the Wotan troopers snapped to attention.

Casually van de Brug touched his good hand to the rim of his rakishly tilted cap, with its tarnished silver skull and crossbones emblem, and strode away.

Kuehn stood the Wotan troopers at ease, as in the doomed city there came the first faint wail of the air-raid sirens. Obviously, Schulze told himself, the Ivans were coming in for another bombing raid. There was nothing to stop the Russian planes, save a little German flak. The *Luftwaffe* had been shot out of the skies.

"All right," Kuehn said, "before I let you go to feed your faces. There's soup and sausage for breakfast this morning and some beer left too."

The faces of the weary, unshaven Wotan troopers brightened at the prospect, as Kuehn continued with, "If we're going to die in this goddamn place, we might as well eat and drink the best. Let me tell you this, however. You might think it strange to be commanded by an American – the enemy. But I'm glad to be here, helping to throw back the Yid-Commie plague while there is still time. I was captured with a group of German-speaking Yids in German uniform – we were on a mission behind German lines – last September. One of the Yids creamed his skivvies and blew the whistle on us. The Germans could have shot me. I was in their uniform after all. But they didn't. They shot the Yids of course." He made the statement as if it was the most obvious thing in the world. "But they gave me the chance of joining the Armed SS. So that's why I'm here, ready to fight to the death, just like any other patriotic German, for Folk, Fatherland and Führer."

He said the last words with energy and resolution, but somehow schulze had a strange feeling that their new commander did not quite mean them.

"All right," Kuehn concluded. "Off you go and get to the trough." He pointed to his right. "It's there among the trees. Dismiss!"

Schulze and the Wotan troopers clicked to attention and Schulze, as senior NCO present, saluted.

Smartly Kuehn returned the salute and then he was gone, striding off briskly in the same direction that van de Brug had taken.

As they walked towards the tented cookhouse, already savouring the aroma of "fart soup", Matz said thoughtfully, "What do you think of our new leader, Schulze? This whole set-up."

For a moment Schulze didn't reply. He was watching a woman who had come out of one of the little tents, hair tousled and blouse unbuttoned, revealing her ample breasts. Without the slightest hesitation she walked over to the nearest tree, pulled down her knickers and directed a stream of hissing yellow urine at the earth. She saw the two NCOs looking at her and said in heavily accented German, "What you look, soldier boys? Never have you seen woman's beaver before?" She laughed coarsely, pulled up her knickers, which were none too clean, and went back inside the tent, from which they now could hear the sound of heavy snoring.

A suddenly worried Schulze rubbed the bristles of his unshaven chin with a hand like a small steam shovel and said, "Not much, Matz, old house. You can easily see that this little lot is a shower o' shit, Christmas tree soldiers, the lot o' em. But those two officers are different. They're sharp and tough and they're up to something, I tell yer that."

Matz looked up at his long-time running mate. "What d'yer mean, Schulze?"

"Look here, birdbrain. You're not the smartest man in the Reich, but even *you* know that Hitler and his frigging lot are kaput, fini, finished. So why do two smartasses like them officers still seem as if they want to fight for Hitler, eh?"

"Well, that cheesehead officer van de Brug said there was no alternative," Matz commented. "They're renegades – an American and a Dutchman – fighting for Germany. All they'd get if they surrendered would be a length of rope."

Schulze shook his head. "Ner, them two is too smart for that," he said firmly. "*They're* not gonna die for any frigging Folk, Fatherland and Führer, you can bet yer life on that. They're up to something." He tapped his forehead significantly. "I just know it up here."

"What?"

Schulze shook his big head. "Who am I – *frigging Jesus*? How should I know. All I know that the two of them are up to something. He sniffed hard. "Come on, there's the cookhouse. Let's stuff a litre of good fart soup down behind our collar studs."

But the two comrades were not fated to eat their "fart soup" just then. They had just entered the dug-in cookhouse, the air inside heavy with the delicious smell of pea soup and sausage, when van de Brug's voice commanded harshly, "*Appell . . . raus . . . everyone out!*"

One of the cooks, an ethnic German it appeared from his accent, dropped his ladle into the big steaming cauldron, and said, "They've caught another one trying to do a bunk. This'll be good." Followed by the other cook, he went out into the open hurriedly.

Schulze and Matz hesitated. Then, grabbing a steaming sausage each from the heaped-up tray, they followed the cooks.

In the clearing in the centre of the tented camp, men of all nationalities – and women too – were forming up in a rough hollow square. They looked dirty and unwashed and were clad mostly in ragged uniforms, which bore plenty of signs of being used for weeks, perhaps months, without ever being cleaned. All their eyes were fixed on the wretched figure in the uniform of the SS with the flash of the *Freikorps Britannien** on the shoulder, who was now being trussed up to a large oak, while Kuehn watched impassively, a riding crop dangling from the loop on his wrist.

Van de Brug cried over the roar of the Russian barrage, "Englishman, you attempted to dessert! For that offence

* British Free Corps, a British section of the SS.

29

I could have you strung up without trial." He paused and looked around the square, making sure that his words were not lost on this motley bunch of soldiers and camp followers. "But I am a generous man and I need everybody I can find for what is to come. So you will not hang, but you must be punished as an example to everyone here of what will happen to them if they attempt to desert. And perhaps next time," the big Dutchman warned, "I might not be so lenient. Kuehn, ten lashes, please."

"*Jawohl*," the American snapped. He strode forward. He snatched at the tied-up man's thin tunic and ripped it and the shirt beneath from him to reveal the skinny, white back.

"Please," the would-be deserter pleaded in a trembling voice, "don't hurt me, I just couldn't stand any more . . ."

His plea was stopped by the crack and stinging lash of the riding crop against his naked back. The man let out an unholy scream. From the tree the rooks rose in hoarse, squawking protest. A thin ugly scarlet line, from which blood was already starting to trickle, suddenly appeared across the Englishman's back.

Now with sudden fury, the big American lashed out again. The prisoner screamed shrilly once more, writhing and twisting, his spine as taut as a bow-string, his hands clenched into fists so that for a moment Schulze thought he was going to burst his bonds. That wasn't to be. Again and again, his face red with the exertion, the American struck the Englishman's bloody back, using all his strength and obviously enjoying his task until finally the prisoner's head lolled to one side, as he fell unconscious. It was only then that Kuehn stopped, his eyes glittering with savage fury, his chest heaving, as if he had just run a great race.

Van de Brug nodded his approval and snapped, "All

right, cut him down. The rest of you go and get your fart soup and nigger sweat." He meant black coffee. "We'll have work to do soon."

The parade broke up and the one-eyed, one-armed Dutch officer swaggered by a suddenly pale-faced Matz and Schulze. "It's rough and tough, I know," he said to the two NCOs. "But it's the only way to keep discipline with a bunch of no-goods like this little lot. Feed 'em, give them their sauce – and carry a big stick." He winked with his good eye and was gone.

Schulze looked at Matz and after he had disappeared said grimly, "By the Great God and all His Holy Triangles, I got us into this frigging mess, Matzi, and I'm gonna frigging well get us out of it, as well. Come on . . ."

# FIVE

The Sixth SS Panzer Army had been retreating ever since March. Week after week the battered remnants of the elite SS armoured divisions – the "Adolf Hitler Bodyguard", the "Death's Head", the "Viking" and the like – had been forced back by the advancing Red Army. The Sixth had fought its way through Hungary, then into Czechoslovakia, and on to Austria, desperately trying to reach the Americans and surrender to them rather than the Russians. For even the simplest SS private soldier knew what would happen to them if they fell into the hands of the "Ivans". Those who wore the insignia of Hitler's elite, that silver skull and crossbones which had once made them the most feared troops in Europe, would be killed instantly.

What was left of SS Assault Regiment Wotan had been scattered among the other shattered formations of the Sixth SS Panzer Army, fighting and retreating, fighting again and retreating once more, with a mixed bunch of troopers from the "Hitler Youth" Division and the "Empire" Division, commanded by unknown officers who usually didn't survive more than a day or so in the bitter, confused fighting of the Hungarian plains and the mountains of Czechoslovakia.

Sergeant Schulze would have none of that. As he had confided to Corporal Matz at the beginning of the retreat,

"*I'm* looking after our little lot," he had snorted, poking a thumb like a hairy sausage at his bread powerful chest. "Heaven, arse and cloudburst, what use to us is some snotty second lieutenant, straight from cadet school, who wouldn't last more than twenty-four hours at the most? Ner, Mrs Schulze's handsome son'll see us through." A statement which had occasioned Matz to snort comtemptuously, "Yer know, you don't frigging well piss out of yer ribs. Yer does it just like the rest o' us."

Thus it was that, after a bitter fire-fight with Slovak rebels who had now changed sides from the German Army to the Russian one, they entered a little Slovak hamlet, all half-timbered farmhouses grouped around the white-painted church with its slate-covered onion tower, and Sergeant Schulze made his mistake. They were busy looting a big farmhouse next to the church, frantically searching for anything to eat and drink, for they had done neither all that long hot April day, when the big woman had come down the stairs (later they learned that her husband had fled with all the rest of the village to the partisans). She been clad in a dressing gown which she had been careless in fastening so that a suddenly very interested Schulze could whisper to Matz hoarsely, "Well yer can see she ain't a true blonde, Matzi!"

"Yer," Corporal Matz agreed, "and I wouldn't mind getting me head between that milk factory of hers. It wouldn't give me any pain at all."

The big, blowsy blonde looked knowingly at the two of them, totally unconcerned, or so it appeared, that the rest of the Wotan troopers were looting her home.

"I don't think yer need a crystal ball to fathom out what she wants," Schulze said, eyeing the blonde standing at the head of the stairs, licking lips which had suddenly gone very dry. "Toss yer for her."

33

As always Matz lost. For when the big noncom used his "lucky coin", as Schulze called it, the little corporal always seemed to lose. "All right, Matzi, you can have a go when I'm finished," Schulze announced as he began to clamber up the stairs to the waiting blonde, "though after she's had a taste of my good German salami," he grabbed the already bulging front of his stained breeches to make his meaning quite clear, "I don't think she'll be much interested in that withered little dick of yours."

"Don't take too frigging long," was Corporal Matz's comment, "I've already got a diamond cutter so bad that it hurts."

"Tough titty, my little garden gnome," Schulze responded unfeelingly as he disappeared into the blonde's bedroom . . .

It was thus that Matz found him five minutes later, naked save for his pistol belt, boots and helmet – "a good soldier's always ready for battle – *or bed* – at all times," Schulze always maintained. His naked haunches were pumping vigorously in and out, as the blonde, also naked, wriggled and giggled with delight as the bed springs squeaked in protest. "Schulze, get yer duds on. There's trouble," Matz said urgently.

"Piss off," Schulze gasped, not stopping for a second. "Can't you see I'm occupied with my fiancée . . .?"

"Schulze," Matz pleaded, "don't arse around. We're in trouble, *serious* trouble."

"Go and play with the frigging five-fingered widow. I don't fancy a threesome today." Schulze continued pumping away at the big blonde who had stopped giggling and was now panting wildly, and whimpering in Slovak between gasps, her naked body lathered in sweat.

"*Schulze!*" Matz yelled at the top of his voice. "There's a frigging general downstairs screaming blue murder and there's Czech partisans down the street! We're in trouble. Do you . . ."

"*Let me finish . . . finish!*" Schulze's desperate appeal ended in a grunt, as Matz took off his helmet and slammed it against his naked buttocks. "Now will you get frigging up!" he cried.

Schulze groaned. "*Gross Gott,*" he moaned sadly. "Best diamond cutter I've had in months and some frigging general has to go and spoil it." He rose reluctantly, as the big blonde opened her eyes, her legs still spread wide apart, and stared up at him puzzled. "*Was ist los?*"* she asked in accented German.

"*Der Teufel ist los, Liebling,*"† Schulze answered. He bent gravely and kissed her calloused hand, as if he were the hero in one of those romantic Viennese movies that were fashionable that year in the Reich. "Madam," he said ponderously, "the trumpet sounds, the drum beats. I must lead my men into battle. But promise me this – remain true to me, my darling, until I return."

Half understanding, the Slovak woman nodded her blonde head and slowly started to lower her legs.

"Knock it off, Schulze," Matz urged. "That general downstairs is a real tough bastard. Fur and blood is going to fly if you don't get down them dancers sharpish."

"All right, all right," Schulze said easily as he began to pull on his trousers while the blonde watched the source of her delights disappearing with a disappointed look on her broad Slavic face. "When has Sergeant Schulze ever been frightened of officers, even a frigging general? Come on, Matzi!"

Now as the two of them clattered down the stairs, they

* "What's up?"
† "The devil is up, darling."

could already hear the angry snap-and-crackle of a fire-fight further down the street and the quick hysterical hiss of a Spandau firing all out. "Frig it," Schulze moaned, "the frigging war's frigging well caught up with us again!"

"What in three devils' name do you think you are about, Sergeant?" the officer, dressed in the black uniform of an SS police general, demanded. "Do you think I've not got all my cups in the cupboard? I know what you've been doing – fornication with a piece of third-class Slavic trash while the enemy attacks, eh!" The police general was a big man with a great overhanging paunch, a typical rear-echelon stallion, Schulze told himself. Now he was caught in the great retreat and for the first time in the whole of the war he was having to earn his pay and he didn't like it one bit.

"I was recceing the position, sir," Schulze lied doggedly, "from an upper window. Unfortunately I must have looked the wrong way. I didn't see the enemy part . . ." He ducked automatically as a rifle bullet shattered the window to his right and pinged off the wall in a spurt of white masonry.

"*Looked the wrong way!*" the big police officer sneered. "All you were recceing was cunt!" He shouted something. Outside a German machine gun started to fire and they could hear the partisans screaming with pain as they ran straight into the hail of bullets being fired by a Spandau at a rate of one thousand rounds a minute.

Schulze realised that there was no way he was going to be able to reason with the fat cop. His hand dropped to the butt of his pistol. Quite calmly he asked, "All right, so what? What are you going to do about it, *Herr General*?"

The bold challenge in Schulze's blue, hard eyes shook the General. He stepped back a pace, as if Schulze might

36

strike him at any moment and blustered, "And what is that supposed to mean, Sergeant?"

"This, *Herr General*." Schulze emphasized the rank again quite contemptuously. "Where in hell's name do you think you are? This is the arsehole of the world. Your kind of bullshit cuts no ice. This is what counts." He slapped his pistol. "This – and nothing else."

The General spluttered. "But this is rank insubordination . . . you can't talk like that to me . . . I'll have you courtmartialled, you big rogue . . . What do you . . ."

He stopped short as Schulze grabbed him by the front of his tunic and pulling his fat face close to his own slablike features hissed, "Go and piss in the wind, *Kumpel*, while you're still in one frigging piece. *Got it?*"

"Why . . . you absolute swine," the General spluttered and stuttered, spittle flying everywhere. "You can't talk to me like that . . . Why, man, don't you realise that I can have the turnip off your shoulders for this – *topped?*"

Schulze flashed a look round the faces of his men. All were bearded and appeared to see nothing. They were at the end of their tether. But they were witnesses. They would all suffer, too, if the rear echelon stallion opposite him reported what he had just said. He whipped out his pistol. It appeared in his big fist as if by magic. "Unbuckle your belt," he ordered.

"What?"

"You heard, tin-ears." He jerked up the muzzle threateningly.

Hurriedly the General undid his belt and dropped his breeches to reveal thin white legs holding up his beer belly.

"Now, I want you to stay there like that for five minutes. The machine gunner can keep the slopeheads at bay that long. Then you can do a bunk."

"Why, why," the General choked in a strangled voice, his face puce with rage. "I'll hound you to the end of the earth for this. You won't escape me. I've got witnesses enough – all these men here."

Calmly Schulze said, pistol still levelled at the General, "You've got to find me first, arse-with-ears."

Twenty-four hours later Schulze volunteered himself and what was left of the company for duty in Berlin – "to protect our beloved Führer to the end". As he said to Matz as they waited for the planes to fly them away from Sixth SS Panzer Army's HQ. "I've dropped us all in the shit, just for the sake of a bit of foreign cunt. But it's the only way, Matz, the only way . . ."

# SIX

Adolf Hitler wept bitterly.

Kneeling next to him on the rumpled bed, Eva Braun, his mistress, stared down at the naked Führer in dismay. She had never seen her lover weep before. He had always been masterful, in charge of events, even at some of the worst moments of the war. She reached out her hand and stroked the back of his dyed hair. "I can try again, little chap," she said softly, using his favourite term of endearment. She got up from the bed and took off her nightdress, leaving herself naked save for the black sheer silk stockings that he liked her to wear for love-making. She glanced at her body in the dressing table mirror and told herself she looked good, even after a week in the underground bunker, without benefit of hairdressers and beauticians.

Hitler looked up, his pale worn face wet with tears. "It's not only that" – gently pushing away her hand as she reached once again for his penis – "that I can't make love. I'm finished, finished altogether."

"Don't say that, *Snuggerl*," she tried to reassure him. "There's always hope. The 25th German Army might relieve Berlin. The Russians and Western Allies might soon fall out. You've always said they would . . ."

She stopped short. She could see that her words of reassurance were having no effect.

Hitler rubbed his knuckles into his eyes like a small child slowly awaking from a bad dream. "One has to be realistic," he said, suddenly very calm – too calm, she told herself. "There is no hope. I shall die here in Berlin." Hitler made the statement calmly, without emotion.

She was shocked, but she heard herself say, "Well, Adolf, if you want to die here, then I shall die with you."

He seized her hand and pressed it to his lips. "Thank you, my beloved Eva," he said. "Now we must get dressed. I shall watch you – for the last time. I have always liked to watch you dress."

"And then?"

"I shall get my affairs in order. But first we must be married. You have been a loyal companion to me for these many years. I wish to make you my wife before the . . ." He didn't complete the sentence.

*"Oh Adolf!"* she exclaimed rapturously, her face animated by almost unbearable emotion. She knew that throughout their relationship the Führer had refused to marry her always because he feared it would diminish his uniqueness as Leader of the German Nation. Now he didn't care.

Now carefully, in a kind of striptease in reverse, she started to put on her clothes. First the black silk panties, wriggling into them, displaying the warm globes of her buttocks to him. Then the bra, bending over so that he had a good view of her excellent breasts before encasing them in the delicate lace cups of the bra, and finally the dress, buttons being closed one by one, teasingly. Finally she was ready and he rose with a little sigh, as if to symbolize that this was the very last time, and started to put on his uniform.

Ten minutes later the group assembled in the map room

40

of the bunker for the wedding ceremony. It was simple enough. Hitler and his bride declared that they were of pure Aryan descent and were free from hereditary disease. In view of the war situation they both declared, too, that they wanted a wartime wedding sealed by simple word of mouth and without any delay.

The two witnesses stepped forward to sign the marriage document. The first one was Dr Goebbels, the diminutive Minister of Propaganda, dragging his club foot behind him. Then came Bormann, his heavy face looking worried and a little frightened. For he knew what this marriage ceremony signified. If Hitler was now letting the world know he was a normal man who had sexual drives, who got married; he was finished. It could be only a matter of hours now and then it would all be over. The time had come for him to leave.

"Champagne!" Hitler ordered after Bormann had signed the marriage document as the second witness. "Bring in the secretaries. All of us will have champagne to celebrate."

Bormann's gloom deepened. The Führer rarely touched alcohol and certainly not in public. The image that the Führer had cultivated for so long, the celibate leader who abhorred meat and alcohol, was crumbling fast. He'd be asking for a thick slice of pork sausage next.

Linge served the ice-cold French wine and after the toasts, Hitler turned to Goebbels and said, "My wife and I choose to die in order to escape the shame of overthrow or capitulation. It is our wish that our bodies be burned immediately in the place where I have performed the greater part of my daily work during the twelve years of service to my people."

Goebbels sprang to his feet. "I, too, shall die here, together with my wife and five children!"

Hitler looked shocked. "You cannot kill your children and Magda, your wife. That would be monstrous, Goebbels. You must leave the bunker with them."

Goebbels' dark, vicious eyes flashed fire. "How can I, as the Defender of Berlin, leave," he ranted, "and leave the troops to their fate? That is unthinkable, *mein Führer*. I refuse to go."

Now Hitler's sallow face flushed angrily. "Not even the most faithful of my followers will obey me," he cried angrily.

Goebbels' eyes flooded with tears. "You must not send me away, my dear Führer," he wailed. "I couldn't stand the shame. Life will have no meaning for me if I cannot spend it in the service of you, *mein Führer*, and at your side."

Bormann had had enough. They were all acting the fool. He had no more time for such histrionics. He had to finalize his own plan of escape while there was still time. Swiftly he walked and pushed his way down the crowded corridors, filled with drunken officers and secretaries as usual. Behind the closed door of the dentist's surgery, there came the hectic squeaking of the dental chair as if the medic was fighting to pull out an obstinate tooth. But Bormann knew that wasn't the case. The dentist was making love in the chair to his blonde assistant once more. He shook his head in mock wonder. They had all gone crazy. Why didn't they get out while there was still time?

He turned into his own little room and closed the door. As always the place stank and the dynamo in the shaft next door was going all out. But Bormann noted neither the stink nor the noise. He had his mind on other much more important things.

He turned on the light and under the single naked bulb

he studied the map of West and Central Berlin which was pinned to one of the walls. A staff officer had brought it up to date only the hour before and he could see from the red pins stuck everywhere that the centre of the capital was almost totally surrounded by the Red Army.

With his nicotine-stained forefinger he traced the escape route still open leading to the west and the German 25th Army, which was supposed to be marching eastwards to relieve the capital, though Bormann doubted if it would ever achieve that aim. It led down the Hermann Goering Strasse, through the Brandenburg Tor, up the Charlottenburger Chaussee, to the Tiergarten railway station. From there the escapers followed the Kantstrasse, which Bormann knew from the reports was already under systematic Russian gunfire, and the Masuren Allee to the headquarters of the Hitler Youth movement where a guide would lead the escaper to the Reichsportfeld. From thence the route led to the German bridgehead at Pichelsdorf where the escaper sailed down the Havel and landed on the western bank between Gatow and Kladow.

Bormann pursed his thick sensual lips thoughtfully. It was a long and difficult route, he told himself, fraught with danger. But it was one he would have to take. There were electric boats near the Pichelsdorf Bridge. They were absolutely silent and would not attract the attention of the Russians nearby. Once he reached them, he'd be safe. Then it would be to Sweden on the Swedish passport already sewn into the uniform he would wear, complete with passports from half a dozen other European and South American countries.

He frowned, barely aware of the drunken noise from outside. A woman was obviously pressed up against the other side of the door to his room. She was gasping excitedly, saying in an excited whisper every now

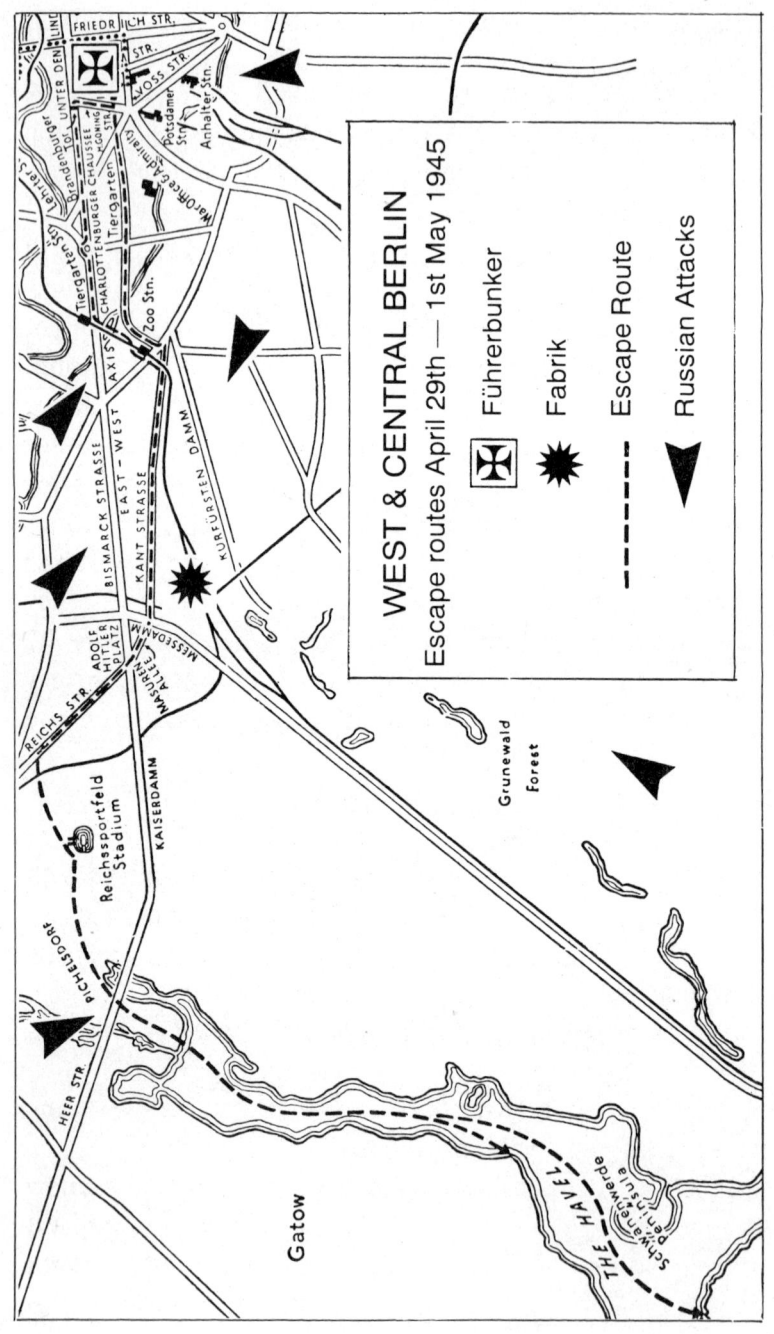

WEST & CENTRAL BERLIN
Escape routes April 29th — 1st May 1945

Führerbunker

Fabrik

Escape Route

Russian Attacks

and again. "Not here, Karl . . . oh please not here, Karl!"

He crossed the little room and locked the door from the inside. The little incident was just one more indication that all discipline had broken down. There wasn't much time left now before the end.

He crossed to his safe and opened it after a few turns of the tumblers and dials. The bullion was already on its way by courier plane to Sweden, where it would go straight into his secret account in the State Bank at Stockholm. But in case of eventualities, unexpected ones, he knew he had to make other provisions. He took out the leather bag filled with diamonds. He weighed it in his hand for a moment. It was hard to believe that such a few stones could be worth nearly a million dollars, but the expert had assured him they were. The gems would be his emergency fund, together with the ten thousand US dollars. Yes, he was well provided for in all senses of the word, courtesy of the Party funds, of which he was in charge, and the German taxpayer.

Outside the woman was whispering urgently, "All right, put it in *quick*! While there's nobody about." Next moment she started to moan passionately and the door rattled with the impact of the man thrusting himself into her body.

Bormann flashed an angry look at the door and was half tempted to open it and discipline whoever was disturbing him like that. But he decided against it. He had other things to do.

"So," he said to himself, "I've got the escape route, the means to do so. What do I need?"

It was a rhetorical question because he already knew the answer to that question. He needed protection. Of course, people broke out from the bunker every night and he could go with such a group. But once he was safe, he wanted to disappear, "take a dive", as they called it. He didn't want to be hampered by officers and officials who knew him. More than likely they would betray him if he said that he wanted to go his own way. No one was safe from treachery this terrible April.

No, he told himself, he needed men who could be bought to protect him, simple soldiers who could be paid off afterwards and would ask no questions about what he was going to do next.

Now the door was rattling furiously and the unknown woman was making great animal sobs of lust and pleasure. "Gutter animals," he snorted to himself angrily. "Rutting in the street like dogs on heat in—" He stopped short abruptly, the pair making love outside his door forgotten totally. *"SS Assault Regiment Wotan,"* he said aloud. Hadn't the Führer said something about their being ferried in just before he had heard of Himmler's treachery?

Bormann was no soldier, but he had heard a lot about the famous – some said infamous – Wotan. Hard and brutal, its men had fought over three continents since the war had commenced, becoming a law unto themselves, caring nothing for the rest of the SS, not to speak of the *Wehrmacht*. Their only loyalty was to their comrades and Wotan.

He rubbed his heavy jowl. They were his. They could be bought. He reached for the phone, the plan unfurling in his brain as he did so as if he had known it all along . . .

# SEVEN

"Cossacks!" Kuehn hissed, as he and van de Brug crouched in the undergrowth, surveying their front through the binoculars. Over central Berlin the Russian Stormoviks, dive bombers, were falling out of the sky, deadly little eggs tumbling from their blue-painted bellies in crazy profusion.

But the two SS officers had no eyes for the renewed air attack now. Their attention was concentrated totally on the riders clattering in single file through the stream that ran through the forest, rifles and tommy guns bumping up and down on their backs.

"They know we're here somewhere," van de Brug whispered as though they might hear him, although they were some two hundred metres away. "Once they locate us, they'll whistle up the infantry and guns."

Kuehn nodded his agreement. It was the usual Russian tactic: send the marauding riders out to recce the enemy positions, draw fire and then report back to the waiting infantry. "Then we'd better liquidate the lot of them," he snapped, lowering his glasses now that they had identified the riders on their shaggy ponies.

In front of the little column, their officer raised his hand to halt the riders and then reached inside his shirt to touch something hanging on a leather thong from his neck. Van de Brug who had fought Cossacks before knew what it was – a little leather bag filled with soil from his native country. It was a Cossack custom. If a Cossack died in battle far from the place of his birth his comrades would sprinkle the bag of earth over him to signify he had died and been buried in his native soil.

"They're about to attack!" van de Brug said urgently. "They know we're in here somewhere. Now they'll try to flush us out." He raised his voice slightly. "Stand to, everybody!" he commanded.

Five metres away, Schulze, dug in with the rest of the Wotan in a line of camouflaged foxholes, repeated the order softly, adding, "And remember those things they're carrying in their mitts are not toothpicks!" He laughed at what he thought was a tremendously witty sally. For his part, Corporal Matz raised his right haunch and ripped off a fart to show his contempt.

"That's dumb insolence, Corporal Matz," Schulze said without rancour. "I could have you for that."

Matz stuck up his middle finger. "Sit on that!" he replied.

"Silence," van de Brug hissed, reaching for his pistol. "Here they come!"

Now they had crossed the stream, the Cossacks, fur hats tilted rakishly to one side, sabres already drawn, were spreading out in a long line, pulling at the bits of their horses, which were frisky and nervous, as if they could already scent the men lying in wait for them in the holes among the bushes. The officer rose in his saddle. "*Slava krasnaya armya!*" he yelled at the top of his voice. "Long live the Red Army!"

"*Slava krasnaya armya!*" A hundred deep bass voices echoed the words in unison.

At the trot, bouncing up and down in their saddles, the

48

riders came on, sabres pointing downwards, ready for the first sight of the German enemy.

"Aim low," van de Brug ordered, a note of rising excitement in his voice. "Get the horses, then the riders. None of them must escape, do you hear?"

*Two hundred metres . . . one hundred and fifty . . . one hundred metres.* The Cossacks were riding at a goodly trot despite the trees, dodging the overhanging branches effortlessly, some of them holding the reins in their teeth so that they had both hands free to wield both sabre and pistol. *Seventy-five metres!*

Van de Brug could wait no longer. The enemy cavalry was almost on the SS positions. He could see the riders quite clearly, tall, bearded men dressed in black, wearing the traditional uniform of the Cossacks with large old-fashioned cartridges sticking out from the pockets on both sides of their coats. "*FIRE AT WILL!*" he yelled above the clatter of steel equipment and the steady drumming of the horses' hooves.

The line held by the SS exploded in violent action. Half a dozen Cossacks were thrown from their horses as if punched by an invisible fist. Horses went down too, flanks suddenly stained a bright scarlet. Some reared into the air, hooves flailing crazily. Others sank to their forelegs, whinnying with pain, trying desperately to fight off death, while their riders cursed and swore, tugging savagely at the bits.

In an instant the forest was transformed into a chaotic scene of murder and mayhem. Cossacks screamed and fell to the ground. Lead hissed through the air like heavy summer rain, Branches crackled and rumbled. Leaves rained down. Horses reared and plunged. Panic-stricken horses galloped away, dragging their dead riders with them by the stirrup. But still the survivors came on with that reckless courage for which the Cossacks were famous.

Now the first of them were within the German lines. They lay about them with their sabres, the silver blades flashing to left and right, their tips stained, suddenly, a blood-red.

Schulze jumped from his hole as a Cossack came at him full tilt, reins in his teeth, a pistol in one hand, a sabre in the other. Schulze pressed the trigger of his machine pistol. *Nothing happened!* He had a stoppage. "Christ on a crutch!" he yelled, as the Cossack, a great pockmarked rogue, grinned when he saw that Schulze was defenceless. He dug his heels into the sweat-gleaming flanks of his stallion, urging it to greater effort. "Sod this for a game of soldiers," Schulze cursed. In one and the same instant he had pulled his last grenade from his boot and had thrown it. Hurriedly he ducked. There was a tremendous flash, followed a moment later by the thick crump of explosive. Horse and rider disappeared into the dark brown smoke for an instant. When it cleared, the horse, its forelegs severed, lay writhing on the churned-up ground, scarlet blood jetting in a bright gleaming stream from the terrible wounds. Next to it lay the dead rider, sword and pistol still clenched in his hands, but minus his head.

Still the survivors came on, leaning far down over the sides of their mounts, hacking away savagely at the infantry. Here and there, the SS broke and fled from their holes. The Cossacks were after them in an instant, hacking at the running men's backs with the razor-sharp sabres like butchers suddenly gone crazy.

But the infantry's fire was taking its toll. More and more of the horses and their riders went down, to be trampled under the flying hooves of those who came after them. "Let no one escape," van de Brug yelled above the frantic noise and confusion of the bloody mêlée, *"not a single one!"* He took careful aim with his pistol, standing bolt-upright as if on some peacetime firing range. He pressed the trigger. A Cossack, galloping straight at him, was propelled from his saddle as if he had been punched by a gigantic fist. His mount galloped on, nostrils distended, eyes wide and wild with fear.

Now the last few surviving Cossacks, some of them on foot, were inside the German lines, being fired upon on all sides. They hadn't a chance. It was no longer war. It was a massacre, as the infantry systematically slaughtered them until finally the last half a dozen still on their feet, threw away their weapons and raised their hands in surrender, crying in broken German, *"Nix schiessen!"* But still the firing didn't let up until they, too, had dropped to the ground, dead or dying. Slowly the firing died away, leaving behind it a loud echoing silence, broken only by the moaning of the wounded. Van de Brug looked at Kuehn. The big American nodded. Together he and van de Brug started to walk around the bodies, kicking those they thought might be shamming death. If the Cossack reacted, the American and the Dutchman placed the muzzle of their pistols at the base of the Russian's skull and blew his head off . . .

Corporal Matz had seen much of war over these last six years, but he had never been able to get used to the slaughter of prisoners in cold blood. Moodily he sipped at the "flatman", a flat bottle of vodka, looted from one of the dead, and watched as Kuehn and van de Brug went about their self-appointed tasks.

Next to him, Sergeant Schulze, also holding a bottle of looted vodka, felt the same. "You can see that big *Ami* likes that sort of thing. Remember how he used that whip on that poor shit the other day."

Matz nodded and said nothing.

Schulze took another slug of the fiery liquid and coughed. "There's something fishy about the two of them altogether."

"You've said that before." Matz broke his silence as van de Brug bent and pumped another slug into the head of a dying Cossack. The skull disintegrated like a soft eggshell tapped by a too-heavy spoon. Bone gleamed like polished ivory in the red gore. "But we're stuck with them. So hold yer noise."

"I don't know about that," Schulze answered softly and thoughtfully, as if speaking to himself. "Well we are – for a while." Then he, too, relapsed into silence.

Half an hour later while they lolled in their slit trenches, waiting for something to happen, smoking moodily and in silence, the signals corporal doubled over to where van de Brug and Kuehn squatted drinking, bearing a message in his hand. He saluted and handed the mesagge to the one-armed Dutchman, He read it quickly and passed it over to Kuehn. His eyes flashed through it. He gave a brief, careful, cold smile and then winked at the other officer as if they were conspirators whose luck was holding out after all.

Schulze watching them, stroking the bristles of his hairy chin, frowned. There was something going on, but what?

Half an hour later, with a soft yellow moon beginning to rise in the evening sky and with van de Brug in the lead, they were ordered to march. "You and your men from Wotan will bring up the rear, Schulze," van de Brug commanded at the briefing. "Herr Kuehn will be in charge of the rear. I'll command the rabble in front and see that they don't try to do a bunk. Clear?"

"Clear, sir," Schulze answered and then asked, "What's our objective, sir?"

Van de Brug shook his head, face revealing nothing save a look of self-satisfaction. "We haven't got an objective on this one." He nodded to the centre of the doomed capital where the sky was as bright as day. "We've been called to the bunker."

"The bunker?" Schulze echoed, puzzled.

"Yes, the Führerbunker. Reichsleiter Bormann has ordered us to make our way there as soon as possible. It's going to be tough, but we can do it."

Five minutes later they were on their way, a long column of men, each man wrapped up in a cocoon of his own fears and apprehensions. Behind they left the slaughtered, stiffening in the sudden cold. No one looked back.

# EIGHT

Van de Brug was first to spot the naked girl, dancing on the kitchen table. She was swaying back and forth, obviously drunk, but still able enough to dodge the hands of the drunken Red Army, who grabbed for her skinny buttocks and teenage buds of breasts. "*Ivans!*" he said and crouched. Immediately the long file of men in the ruined street did the same, nerves tingling electrically, trigger fingers clenched.

They had been going nearly two hours now. Once or twice they had come under Russian fire, but it had been some way off and they had dodged it easily. Now it seemed, as they watched the wild gyrations of the drunken teenager, who couldn't have been a day older than fourteen, they realised they had run into the enemy forward line. And everywhere the place was as light as day in the lurid flames of burning houses. It took only one glance backwards by the Russian packing the house where the girl danced and they would be for it.

Van de Brug bit his lip. What was he going to do? It was only a matter of metres before they could slip into the sewers that led under the Russian positions, encircling the centre of Berlin. He made his decision. "All right," he hissed to the man behind him, "pass it back. We're going to make a dash for it. It's every man for himself. Fire at anybody not wearing a German uniform." He clicked off his safety catch.

In the ruined house, a small swarthy soldier had sprung onto the table and was mimicking the girl's every obscene gesture to the delighted whistles and cheers of his comrades. The drunken girl was enjoying the attention. She pushed her pelvis ever closer to that of the young Russian, sweat streaming down her lithe young body. Van de Brug prayed to God that the Ivans would be so fascinated by the sexual performance that they would not notice his men sneaking by. "*Los!*" he said and clapped the nearest soldier on the back. "Go!" And all the time he kept his one eye fixed on the room as if hypnotized.

Now a dozen men had passed and were assembling next to the grating which led down to the great sewers that flowed beneath Berlin. Somewhere down there the guide would be waiting for him. But not for long. Van de Brug knew it was imperative to get down there soon and contact him, greasing palms with gold coins and cigarettes. It was the only way the besieged Berliners were prepared to do business these days.

On the table the little Russian was trying to take his clothes off, his intentions pretty obvious, and dance at the same time. Wildly the others cheered and clapped, the war forgotten. Suddenly disaster struck. The Russian stumbled and fell backwards, breeches still around his knees, his erection sticking out like a club under his brown shirt. The girl, taken by surprise, fell from the table, too, right into the lap of a surprised sergeant.

Van de Brug hesitated no longer. He pressed the trigger of his pistol. The fat sergeant pitched forward, shirt suddenly stained a deep red, carrying the screaming naked girl with him.

Pandemonium broke out immediately as the Russians

spotted the men in field grey trying to sneak by their positions. Tracer zipped wildly through the air. Bombs exploded. Somewhere an ancient Russian machine gun began tapping away like a slow, angry woodpecker.

Now the escapers were running all out down the ruined street, the bricks of the shattered walls glowing a lurid crimson. In the rear, Kuehn gasped, "Down the parallel street! They must have spotted the rest up front. We can break through one of the houses lower down to reach the sewers."

Schulze needed no urging. "Follow me," he cried above the racket, "the captain's got a hole in his arse." Together they all pelted down the cobbled road, Matz, with his wooden leg, keeping up as best he could. Schulze burst into a house. A naked Russian, towel over his shoulder, was standing in a bowl washing himself. Schulze fired. A red hole appeared in the man's pale yellow belly. He stared down at it, as if wondering how the hole got there. Then he fell to his knees in the bowl, the water turning a bright red. Schulze kicked him cruelly in the face as he raced by him.

Another Russian surprised Schulze by coming out of a side door. There was no room to use his pistol. He reacted instinctively. He hooked his two fingers into the man's nostrils and pulled hard. The flesh broke. Blood flooded his fingers. He let go. The Russian reeled away, clutching his shattered nose. Schulze ran on.

He slammed through a door. A machine gun opened up. Behind him the Englishman who had tried to desert screamed shrilly. He flung up his hands as if he were climbing the rungs of an invisible ladder. Moments later he pitched forward on his face, dead before he hit the cobbles. Matz fired. The Russian tommy-gunner went down.

Now the two old comrades could see the men urgently jostling to get down the iron ladder into the sewers, while Russian lead cut the air all around them. There were already half a dozen soldiers in field grey lying still on the ground next to the opening or writhing in pain.

Kuehn shouted. "Get your Wotan fellows into the shaft! They're important. This lot" – he indicated the Turcomans who presumably couldn't speak German – "will hold the ground. We can afford to lose them."

Schulze didn't hesitate. He knew time was running out – *fast*. "Wotan on me," he bellowed above the bitter snap-and-crackle of the fire fight. He placed his hand on his helmet, fingers splayed, the infantry signal for "rally on me".

"Come on!" Kuehn shouted. "Let the Chinks get on with it!" He yelled angrily as a bullet smacked into the wall near his head, showering his helmet with bits of brick. They began to run. Schulze felt a slug tear off the heel of his boot. Another slug slammed into Matz's wooden leg and the little corporal yelled, "Frig this, they're turning me into firewood!"

Schulze jumped over a dead SS man, the back of his head blown off. Just ahead him was the dark shaft, from which an awesome stench came. "God in heaven!" he cried. "Just like attar of roses." He grabbed a panting Matz and put him on the first rung of the dark ladder leading downstairs and warned, "Don't frigging well slip, Matzi, or yer'll be up to yer hooter in crap. *Move it now!*"

Matz moved it.

Up above, covering his men, Schulze swung from left to right like a western gunslinger in a wild west film hosing the street with slugs, as the Russians dodged into the doorways, frustrated in their attempts to finish off the Germans still remaining above the surface of the ground.

"All right," Kuehn snapped. "After me, Schulze, the rest'll have to look after themselves. The devil take the hindmost." He dropped into the shaft. Schulze followed, still firing. A moment later he dropped the hatch lid behind him and fastened it, gagging at the stench coming from below.

A burst of machine-gun fire followed them through the grill. A Wotan trooper screamed shrilly. He tumbled to the bottom of the ladder and fell into the evil-smelling water with a splash. Matz grabbed him and pulled him out and laid him on a sort of concrete platform which ran to both sides of the central canal under the sloping roof of the sewer.

It was Dietz, one of the "old hares", who had survived Russia and Monte Cassino. He was chewing his tongue in pain and the saliva which ran down his unshaven chin was tinged pink with blood. He had been badly hit. His eyeballs were already beginning to turn upwards so that only a tiny slit of white showed. Still, he was conscious.

"Leave him," Kuehn ordered. "He's had it."

Schulze pushed the big American to one side. "I'll decide who we leave," he growled. "Gimme a knife somebody."

Someone handed him a bayonet. Carefully Schulze slid the blade in between the grinding teeth. Immediately Dietz's breathing improved as Schulze levered the teeth apart and raised the tongue. Schulze sat back on his heels, telling himself that he had saved old Dietz's life. He was mistaken.

"Look at this, Schulze," Matz said, pulling his hand from beneath Dietz's tormented body and holding it up. It was covered in blood. "He's been shot down below."

Suddenly Schulze was aware that the stench was not

only coming from the sewer, but also from the wounded man's body. "Pull his pants down," he ordered.

Matz did so.

The soldier's trousers were full of yellow blood. Gently Matz turned him over. Blood was spurting thickly from his anus and lower back.

"Christ on a crutch," Schulze cursed. He grabbed a handful of mud and packed it against the wound. Still the blood leaked through in seconds.

Kuehn hesitated no longer. He pulled out his pistol. Before Schulze could stop him, he placed the muzzle against Dietz's head and pulled the trigger. The back of Dietz's head erupted in a welter of red gore, splashing Schulze's boots and flinging shattered bone through the glowing darkness of the sewer.

"*Why you swine!*" Schulze exploded. "You didn't give him a chance . . ."

"He didn't have a chance," Kuehn interrupted him harshly. "And don't talk to me like that, Sergeant," he added threateningly. "This is my kind of discipline." He jerked up the muzzle of his pistol. "Now come on, let's move."

Schulze hesitated, fists balled up in anger. He looked down at Dietz's poor shattered head and he growled. But Matz dug him in the ribs hard. "Come on, Schulze," he whispered. "You can't bring him back to life now."

Schulze nodded glumly and then he moved into the sewer, joining the others to wade up to his ankles in the flowing filth, while above the frustrated Russians hammered at the hatch, firing wild bursts through the grille.

Then they turned round a bend and the Russians were left behind. Ahead they saw, in the light of a flickering yellow lantern, an old man clad in waders with a strange-looking leather helmet on his head. It was their guide. He had waited for them after all.

"Well, the head shit-shoveller's there at least," Matz said, nose wrinkled at the awesome stench of the sewer. "Let's hope he can get us through this little lot, toot-sweet. I can't stand much more of this pong."

"It's better than a Russian bullet in your heart," Kuehn commented. "Now button up your lip and keep silent."

# NINE

With the old man with his smelly carbide lantern swinging from side to side in the lead, they advanced ever deeper into the main sewer. Now the rats were everywhere. Whether it was due to the fighting above ground or because of the growing darkness, Matz couldn't tell. All he knew was that the loathsome creatures were there in their hundreds, perhaps thousands, fleeing the flickering light of the old man's lantern, but slithering under his feet again once it had vanished.

"Ugh!" Matz complained to a strangely silent Schulze. "Gives me the creeps to feel the long-tailed bastards nibbling at me feet – even at my wooden leg."

Schulze didn't respond and Matz relapsed into silence again, as did all the rest of the escapers. Each was assailed by an uneasy feeling that the Russians up above would trace their route, just waiting for an opportunity to attack them. For, at regular one hundred metre intervals, there were patches of light from shafts which had been built to allow rainwater to run off into the main sewer. Twice there had been bursts of fire into these shafts, as they had scrambled and splashed hurriedly to the safety of the sewer beyond.

Time passed. Half an hour after they had entered the sewer, the wrinkled, yellow-faced old guide held up his finger to his lips and whispered, "Ivan barricade ahead just round the bend. Have to pass it one by one. And for God's sake, don't make the slightest noise. The Ivans have got the barricade covered. All right, let's go."

With the guide standing in the shelter of the curved wall, his lantern darkened, van de Brug went first, crawling through a confused mess of old chairs, ration crates, rolls of barbed wire and the like which the Russians had thrown down the shaft to prevent anyone using the sewer. The others watched anxiously as the one-armed officer made his way through, bodies tensed for the first angry cry of alarm and the burst of tommy gun fire. But van de Brug made it without incident and waved for the next man to make the attempt.

One by one, lathered in sweat and not daring to make the slightest noise, the escapers worked their way through the barricade to group on the other side to watch the next SS man come through.

Schulze and Matz, waiting their turn with the rest of the rearguard, knew the Russians were up there all right. During lulls in the gunfire above they could hear voices speaking in Russian and once a glowing object had come tumbling down the shaft – for one anxious moment they had thought it was the burning fuse of a bomb – and dropped into the sewer, where it hissed and went out. A Russian cigarette end! All of them breathed a sigh of relief.

Then it was Matz's turn. "Here, give me yer popgun," Schulze said, taking Matz's Schmeisser. "You've got enough problems with that peg-leg of yours, apeturd." But there was a note of worry in his tough voice.

"Give me a quick kiss before I go," Matz whispered and made a wet, kissing noise.

"Move it!" Kuehn hissed angrily.

Cautiously Matz started to fight his way through the

mess of the barricade, hampered by the stiff wooden leg. It was tough going for the little man and Schulze watched his progress with growing anxiety. He was making terribly slow work of it. It only needed a Russian to peer through the grating above and he would spot the little corporal worming his way through the chairs and barbed wire.

Then it happened. A harsh voice in Russian challenged, "*Stoi?*"

Matz froze in the barricade, as that harsh Russian challenge echoed and re-echoed around the chamber.

Schulze gripped the trigger of his machine pistol.

"*Nemetzki!*" – the Germans – the Russian up above shouted.

Schulze acted instinctively. "All right, the rest of you get across. I'll tackle the Ivans." Without waiting to see if they were reacting to his order, he pressed the trigger of the Schmeisser. A shrill scream came from up above. A deafening chatter. Slugs flying everywhere and then the others were scrambling through the barricade frantically, dragging Matz with them, as Schulze braced himself against the cover of the sewer wall waiting for what came next before making his own attempt to get through.

A stick grenade came trundling down trailing a series of angry red sparks behind it. It hit the sewer floor. Schulze didn't hesitate. He aimed a mighty kick at the grenade. It went flying into the sewer some fifty metres away and exploded in a thunderous roar, splitting the gloom with a vivid burst of scarlet flame and throwing up a wild, white spout of angry water.

Then Schulze was running, splashing through the water of the sewer, heading for the barricade before the Russians reacted once more.

More time passed. One of the men who had been

wounded passed out and sank into the nauseating mire which was now up to their boot tops. Van de Brug ordered him pulled up. Belts were taken off and tied about the man's arms. Thus they dragged the faeces-smeared man behind them, faces set in a look of absolute disgust.

"Another half kilometre to the German lines." The words passed from man to man as the long line fought its way through the sewer. "Another half a klick. Pass it on."

"Thank God!" Matz grunted with relief. Now he had a dirty handkerchief tied around his mouth and nose in a vain attempt to keep out the stench. "This place stinks worse than your feet when you take off yer socks each Christmas, Schulze."

Schulze grunted something but didn't comment. He was too preoccupied with the problem of Lieutenant Kuehn and what he and van de Brug were up to. It was pretty obvious now, he told himself, that the big American was a ruthless killer who would stop at nothing to obtain his objective, but what was that objective?

Schulze bit his bottom lip with frustration. It was clear that the two foreign officers had not hesitated one moment to obey the order to march into the centre of the city, which was obviously a death trap. When everyone else was trying to save his skin, now that the war was almost lost, why were the two of them so eager to stick their necks out and have them chopped off? Was it something to do with the Führerbunker? If so, what?

Up front the old guide was telling van de Brug, "This grating up there was called 'piss corner' because there was a horsedrawn cab station up there in the street. On winter mornings the piss used to come down in streams, litres of it." The old man chuckled fondly at the memory.

Van de Brug shook his head, and said, "Old man, can't you think of anything but shit and piss?"

Again the old man chuckled again and said without rancour, "Piss and shit make the world go round, sir. Without them nothing would grow. Without piss and shit we wouldn't eat."

The one-armed SS officer pulled a face and gagged a little at the combination. He opened his mouth to reprimand the old guide, but changed his mind when he saw the shadow reflected on the wall of the tunnel just round the bend they were coming to. Someone was standing there. He held up his arm urgently and hissed, "*Freeze!*"

They stopped as one, hearts suddenly thudding madly, weapons at the ready, the awesome stench of the sewer forgotten immediately.

Pulling out his pistol, van de Brug edged himself out of the slime and onto the narrow ledge which ran to the left of the open sewer. Carefully and slowly he started to edge his way along it, pistol in hand, side pressed against the wall so as to present the smallest possible target. Schulze nodded his approval. Whatever he was up to, the Dutchman was certainly brave. If anyone was waiting for them round that bend, van de Brug was going to be the first target.

He came to the bend. The shadow of a man was being reflected from above onto the wall of the tunnel and the shadow held the war's most frightening weapon – a flame-thrower. A Russian was standing above the grating waiting for them to attempt to pass when he would hose them with that terrible flesh-eating gun!

Van de Brug bit his bottom lip. What should he do? Even as he posed the question to himself he knew the only answer to it. They would have to make a run for it. In the meantime, some of them would fire upwards in the hope that their slugs might ricochet off the walls and knock out the man holding the flame-thrower. Swiftly he explained his plan to the man behind him and snapped, "Pass it on – quick!"

The man, his face suddenly white and ashen, did so. In seconds, everyone in the strung out column knew what was in store for them. They were being expected to run a terrible gauntlet of fire. "Close up," van de Brug ordered.

They shuffled ever closer, those at the rear in Kuehn's group telling themselves that when their turn came the Russians would be waiting for them, but knowing there was no other way out of the trap.

Van de Brug raised his pistol and pointed the muzzle at the flickering shadow on the wall. "*NOW!*" he bellowed, the tunnel echoing and re-echoing with the sound. "*RUN FOR IT!*" He fired the next instant.

Now the first group surged forward almost in panic, filling the sewer from side to side. It was each man for himself, as up above a challenge rang out. Next moment there was a savage hiss like some primeval monster drawing a great fiery breath. A hush. A roar. An angry tongue of evil blue flame shot into the sewer. It curled along the walls, seeking out its victims greedily. An SS man was caught in that all-consuming flame. "*Duck!*" van de Brug yelled frantically. "*Duck under the shit!*" But it was already too late. The cruel flames were already tearing away at the man who had fallen to his knees, screaming piteously as the charred flesh dripped in great strips from his arms and face until finally he flopped forward into the mess, his struggles getting weaker by the second.

Again van de Brug fired a salvo of shots at the shadow on the wall. They howled about the chamber and pinged off the steel grating, but still the shadow remained obstinately standing. He cursed and thrust home a new magazine. "Second group get ready!" he yelled, nostrils now

full of the stink of charred human flesh. "One . . . two
. . . three *GO!*" He fired a whole burst as his terrified
men bolted forward, fighting and tugging at each other
to get to the other side first.

Again that terrible flame-thrower roared. Once more the
horrifying, hissing, vicious tongue of flame sought out its
victims. The air trembled. Standing with the last group,
waiting to make a run for it, Schulze felt himself gasping
and choking for breath. The very air was being sucked
violently from his lungs. The sour stench of burning
flesh assailed his nostrils as men went down everywhere,
screaming, caught by that terrible flame. Others flung
themselve into the stinking mire, burying themselves in
it desperately . . . Then the flame was gone and they
were left fighting their way out of the baked yellow crust
of faeces.

Van de Brug wiped the sweat off his brow. "All right,
Kuehn, it's your group's turn now. Good luck. I'll bring
up the rear. Are you ready?"

"Yessir." Kuehn's voice was firm and determined. He
wasn't afraid, the swine. Schulze could see that. He turned
to the Wotan troopers, bunched together, tensed and
waiting to go. "Remember the old motto," he snapped.
"March or croak! *Ready.*"

Van de Brug fitted the last magazine into his pistol. Once
more he aimed at the shadow on the tunnel wall and cried,
"Los!" He fired.

Then they were all running full out, arms working like
pistons as they pelted for safety. Suddenly there was a
scream. On the wall the shadow crumpled to its knees.
The flame-thrower operator had been hit. Instead of searing
the tunnel, the flame leapt upwards as, in his last dying
moment, the Russian pressed the trigger for one last time.
Schulze yelled triumphantly. "We've done . . . we've done

it!" he exclaimed, as all around him the weary Wotan men, tiredness forgotten for a moment, cheered and cheered.

Fifteen minutes later they paused as above them the sewer cover was opened and an unknown voice said in German, "They're here." Then whoever it was smelt the dreadful odour they gave off and cried, "Phew, give 'em room, boys . . . make way for the shit-shovellers!"

Schulze grinned.

# TEN

Naked and relieved, they stood in the factory courtyard,
ignoring the rumble of gunfire and the occasional Soviet
dive-bomber falling out of the burning sky over central Berlin to release its deadly bombs on the German
defences. Volunteers, wearing gas masks against the
stench of the piles of abandoned uniforms, were sluicing
them down with hosepipes and watering cans.

The Wotan troopers had already had their turn. Now
they lounged in the weak April sun, looking a little puzzled
and wondering what was going to happen next. Sergeant
Schulze soon enlightened them. Still naked himself, he
returned from inside the battered factory which now
served as a battalion HQ. With a grin, he said, "Hide
those little dongs of your'n. I don't want anybody to
know that there are men in Wotan whose dicks look as if
they have been docked by a drunken rabbi." He grinned
and the Wotan troopers grinned back. This was the old
Schulze, trying to defuse the tension of those terrible hours
they had spent in the sewer.

Schulze lowered his voice. "Corporal Matz's inside sorting out some uniforms for you. They've been taken from
the dead, but they've been deloused." He looked to left
and right guardedly, and added, "Don't pick a tunic with
the SS runes and armband. Do you understand, lads?"

They did. Soon anyone found in the uniform of the SS

69

would have a very short life expectancy, once he fell into the hands of the Russians.

He pointed to the blood group marking tattooed under his own brawny arm, which marked a man as belonging to the SS. "As soon as we can we'll get rid of these as well. They say you can remove it with a hot spoon. All right, off you go and cover those disgraceful little love-tools of yours before we become the laughing stock of the *Wehrmacht*."

Hastily the men went inside, leaving Schulze, still naked, standing there staring up at the window of the room where Kuehn and van de Brug were conferring with the local battalion commander. The Dutchman and the American were still in their filthy, stinking uniforms. They had not changed because, for reasons of their own, they had been only too eager to talk to the infantry major. Now Schulze watched as Kuehn handed a bundle of notes to the officer who tucked them smartly away inside his tunic, before pointing to a small civilian truck which was covered by a camouflage net in the corner of the courtyard.

Schulze saw Kuehn nodding his head as if in approval and a few moments later a soldier armed with a Schmeisser came clattering down the stairs and placed himself in front of the vehicle, as if guarding it.

Schulze tugged the end of his long nose. Still naked, he strolled over to the guard with apparent casualness in case the three officers in the room above were watching, and said out of the side of his mouth, "What gives, pal?"

The guard, a mere boy, face pale and set under the big helmet which was two sizes too large for him, said, "I'm not supposed to say. The battalion commander said so."

Schulze forced a laugh. "Who cares about frigging officers?" he said. "I shit officers before breakfast, *mate*. It's the poor frigging stubble-hoppers like us who allus

70

end up with their hooters deep in the crap – not them, *mate*."

The boy nodded his head. "You're right there – er, mate." Obviously he liked being called "mate" by this tough-looking veteran with a thing dangling from between his legs like that of a stallion. "The one with the one eye and one flipper, he gave me twenty cig – er – lung torpedoes and told me to keep a sharp lookout on the truck, mate."

"But what do they need a truck for?" Schulze persisted.

The boy shrugged. "Search me, mate—" The boy's eyes flashed a sudden warning. Someone was coming down the stairs. Hastily Schulze moved towards the room where the uniforms of the dead lay, just as van de Brug and Kuehn came into sight chatting animatedly together, obviously in high good humour. Van de Brug caught sight of the naked giant and said, "You're going to catch a cold like that, Sergeant. Better get some clothes on. Besides, we've got some ladies of the night coming in soon to entertain you coarse stubble-hoppers. Wouldn't like them to see that salami of yours. Put them right off." He laughed at his own humour and started stripping off his filthy tunic, which he followed with his shirt, then unstrapped his wooden arm. "All right, Kuehn," he commanded, "turn on the hosepipe . . ."

"All right, gentlemen – I use the term loosely, you understand – the gash is being sent in in fifteen minutes. I'll give you a toast." He ran his eyes around their faces, white, yellow, and in one case, brown beneath a turban bearing the badge of the SS – a volunteer from the Indian Legion probably, he told himself. He raised the chamberpot filled to the brim with good Munich beer. "Up the cups, lads.

The night's gonna be cool. *Prost!*" Even before the others had raised the mugs, cans and other drinking vessels they had found somewhere, Schulze was guzzling the beer as if he had not drunk anything in ages.

For fifteen minutes solid they drank, each glass or mug or can being followed by a swift slug of fiery schnapps until their faces were glowing and sweating in spite of the coolness of the large open machine shop, where every window was smashed. Eyes sparkled now. They made jokes, not very witty ones, but the kind of sex jokes that soldiers always make on such occasions – "You know what's the second thing that a soldier does when he comes home to his little wifey? Why, *he takes off his pack!*" . . . "Take a last look at the floor, my little darling, 'cos you're gonna be looking at the ceiling for the next forty-eight hours, ha, ha!" – and these supposedly witty sallies were greeted by great bursts of laughter, as if they were the funniest jokes in the world.

They sang, too. Dirty songs, naturally, bellowed in an untuneful baritone. "*Tante Hedwig, Tante Hedwig, meine Nachmaschine, die geht nicht. Ich habe die ganze Nacht probiert und mein ganzes Oel verschmiert . . .*"

And all the while they drank: beer and schnapps, schnapps and beer, so that by the time they heard the first high heels clattering up the steps to the big shop floor, the Indian's face had turned green and his turban was beginning to slip foolishly to one side of his head, and several of the Turcomen, who couldn't tolerate alcohol because as Moslems they were not used to it, were lying face downwards in pools of stale beer.

But Schulze was sober – he was too randy to let himself get drunk. Now as he heard the sound of high heels, he put his two fingers in his mouth and shrilled for silence. The laughter and the singing died away and Schulze bellowed,

72

"Let's have a bit of hush in the knocking shop. All right, they'll be in here in half a sec. I know they're pavement pounders" – he meant whores – "but I don't want any of you perverted asparagus Tarzans to get any fancy ideas," he warned. "The CO tells me he's paid them for a straight little number. None of yer once round the world and can I pop this lollipop somewhere, got it?"

"Got it, Oberscharfuhrer," those who spoke German roared back with drunken enthusiasm.

"*Gut.* Then let the mattress polka begin."

The door burst open and in rushed the pavement pounders, drunk themselves and eager, as if they were still virgins impatient for rape. They were all sizes, shapes and ages. Raddled old blondes who might well have serviced the Kaiser's troops in the Old War; teenagers in white blouses and dark skirts plus white knee socks of the German Maidens, the Hitler Youth organization, amateurs earning cigarette money; strident ladies with cropped hair, corsetted waists and knee-high topboots, who looked as if they might have a whip concealed somewhere about their persons.

"*GASH!*" the drunken soldiers cried as one. "*FEMALE GASH* . . . Hurrah, hurrah, hurrah!" They rose from their tables, scattering chairs and beer glasses in their haste, for all of them knew their lives were going to be short and brutish. This might be the last chance ever.

The mass coupling started immediately; on tables, underneath them, against walls leaning against the rusty, bullet-chipped machinery, in the latrines – anywhere where there was a flat enough space for the whores to lie on their backs and spread their legs.

Naturally Sergeant Schulze, being Sergeant Schulze, had found the best spot of all, a little cupboard-sized bunk bed room just off the factory floor. Perhaps it had once belonged to the night watchman. Now, for a half-hour at least, it was Schulze's kingdom. Matz had protested. "But it's got two beds. I could use the upper one at least."

"Fart in the wind," had been Schulze's reply. "I need two beds, one in use, one for holding the reserve whore. *Gross Gott*, I've got so much ink in my fountain pen, I don't know who to write to first." Then with a gasp of absolute delight, he had pushed the blonde whore onto the bunk, dropped on top of her, boots and all, the wooden bed squeaking dangerously under his great weight and commenced to dance "the mattress polka".

The bombs caught the soldiers completely by surprise. Suddenly, startlingly, they came whizzing down, making the building tremble like a theatre backdrop. Masonry came tumbling down. A gas main exploded. A gigantic blowtorch of searing flame shot upwards. The whores panicked and screamed and fled for cover naked. Soldiers, still erect, ran after them yelling for them to come back.

A bomb hit the rear of the building where half a dozen of the younger whores had huddled together, sobbing, for protection. The wall blew in. Shrapnel and bricks flew through the air in crazy profusion. The girls hadn't a chance. The building was full of the dying screams as fist-sized chunks of red-hot shrapnel sliced their young bodies to pieces, leaving behind a bloody, gory mess of severed limbs and lumps of steaming red flesh so that it all looked like those prewar heaps of offal that butchers left outside their doors of a morning to be collected by the dog food manufacturers.

Schulze forgot his sexual pleasure. He rose and stuffed his shirt back in his breeches. Outside the air-raid sirens were sounding the all-clear. The Soviet dive-bombers were departing. He hurried across the shop floor, automatically

74

noting that all his Wotan troopers had survived the surprise attack, though one or two of them had suffered flesh wounds.

Together with some other soldiers he wrenched at the fallen bricks and masonry to free the bodies. But there was little they could do for the mangled, naked bodies. They were all dead, every single one of them.

"I heard them screaming," one of the whores muttered, watching the sweating, panting soldiers as they worked. "It was awful. If there were a God, he would have shown some mercy on them, even if they were only whores."

Next to her, another "pavement pounder", hard faced, dry eyed, who looked half mad in the eerie, flickering red light of the fires which had broken out everywhere in the bombed factory, turned on her and rasped harshly, "Leave frigging God out of this, woman. God doesn't make wars. *Men* do!"

An hour later, sullen and subdued, the men avoiding each other's gaze, Battle Group van de Brug set off in the red-glowing night on the next stage of their march into the unknown. Bringing up the rear with what was left of the Wotan troopers, Schulze said apropos of nothing, speaking to no one in particular, "Buy combs, lads, there's lousy times ahead . . ."

# PART TWO

# *The end of Berlin*

"Crap, said the King, and a thousand arses bent and took the strain for in those days the word of the King was law."

*The Sayings of Sergeant Schulze*

# ONE

The afternoon of Sunday, April 29th, 1945 was spent in morbid preparations in the Führerbunker. With tears in his eyes, Hitler stroked his favourite dog, the Alsatian bitch Blondi, for the very last time. Then without a word, he handed the lead to the doctor who would poison the dog and turned away. Tamely the Alsatian went with its murderer, as from the upper level came two single shots, as Hitler's two other dogs were put down.

Then Hitler received his secretaries. By now his eyes were glazed and the young women who had served him so loyally throughout the war wondered if the Führer were drugged. Solemnly he shook each one of them by the hand – there was a lot of handshaking this Sunday – and then gave each one of them a poison capsule. "It's a poor parting present," Hitler said. "But if you are taken by the Red beasts, it is better to do away with yourself than suffer what they will do to you, as they have already done to so many decent, honest German women." With that he dismissed them and they wandered off, wondering what they should do, now the pressure was off.

It was about that time that Hitler received yet even more bad news. His fellow dictator, the Italian *Duce*, Mussolini, and his mistress Clara Petacci had fallen into the hands of Italian partisans. They had lynched the two of them and their bodies had been suspended by the feet in the market place in Milan to be beaten and pelted by the jeering, hysterical mob.

Hitler's hand shook badly as he handed the message back to the radioman who had brought it. "My God," he breathed and mopped his brow shakily with a silk handkerchief. "What a fate!" He turned to the crowd around him and said, with sudden firmness in his voice, "When *we* go, I want our bodies destroyed so that nothing remains. Is it that clearly understood?"

The courtiers and hangers-on nodded silently.

"I will not fall into the hands of an enemy who requires a new spectacle to divert his hysterical masses." He breathed out hard and then, turning, walked back slowly to his own apartments.

When he left the others discussed his departure for a while. They agreed that it could signify only that Hitler had made his decision; he was going to kill himself. Suddenly something unexpected happened. A heavy cloud that had oppressed them ever since they had entered the bunker a week before rolled away. The man who had dominated their lives, their every move, for years would soon be gone. The melodramtic tension vanished. For a few brief moments in this twilight of the Third Reich they could play. In the canteen where the soldiers and orderlies ate their meals, a spontaneous dance started. Generals, SS and Army, attracted by the gramophone music, came into the canteen and joined in, doing the foxtrot with secretaries and counter assistants. A party mood spread throughout the bunker, save in Bormann's tight little room.

There he was rapping out some of his last orders in the Führer's name to *Sturmbannführer* Guensche, Hitler's gigantic adjutant, and *Sturmbannführer* Kempka, Hitler's chauffeur. "The Führer will soon take his own life," he rasped, "that is clear. As much as we love and admire him, there is nothing we can do to stop him."

The two SS men looked grave. Kempka was angry, too. He detested Bormann and now he felt that the Party Secretary should do something to prevent the Führer taking his own life. But he kept his mouth firmly closed. Bormann was all powerful and dangerous, too, now that he was virtually in charge.

"I want you two to arrange for – say – two hundred litres of petrol to be placed in the Chancellery garden. The petrol will be used to – er" – he frowned as if even he found it distasteful to say the next words – "to burn the body of the Führer, and his wife's too, of course."

The gigantic adjutant kept control of himself, saying, "But *Herr Reichsleiter*, it will be difficult to find that amount of petrol in here."

Bormann frowned up at him from behind his little desk. "It must be found, *Sturmbannführer*," he snapped severely.

"There's about 40,000 litres buried in the Tiergarten Park," Kempka volunteered. "But it would be death to try to get it during the hours of daylight. The Ivans' artillery is zeroed in on the Park."

"I can't wait that long," Bormann said and bent down to his papers, as if the interview was already over. "See to it."

The two SS officers looked at each other, then clicked to attention, turned and went out.

Bormann looked up immediately, his face wreathed in a self-congratulatory smile. Everything was going according to plan. In twenty-four hours Hitler would be dead; Goebbels probably, too. Then he would be in charge, able to do as he pleased. By then the van de Brug group would be at the Führerbunker and would provide the escort he needed till he reached the Havel and the electric boats. Then he'd give van de Brug a thousand dollars of his "mad money", as he called it, to give to the men or do as he pleased with. With the German currency now virtually absolutely useless a single dollar would be worth a fortune just it had been back in 1923 during the Great Inflation when he had first joined the Party. Thereafter, he'd disappear to Sweden.

He walked over to the closet and opened it. There hung the full uniform of a major-general in the *Waffen SS*. He was entitled to the rank, but he rarely wore the uniform. But tomorrow he would because it would give him the rank and authority he might need during the escape. Thereafter, he would wear the fine English suit which was already packed in his escape rucksack.

He beamed at his pudgy face, with the heavy pugnacious jaw, in the little mirror on the wall and said, "Everything's going to plan, Martin . . . everything."

There was a knock on the door. Swiftly he closed the door of the closet and slid behind the desk as if even now he was immersed in Party affairs. "*Herein*," he snapped in his most official manner.

It was Heidi, one of his female teleprinter operators. She had been crying; her childlike, pale face was still stained by tears. In her hands she held a message.

"Yes?"

"Message for you, *Herr Reichsleiter*, secret and personal."

He took it and she turned as if to go out, but he said, feeling a sudden surging of his loins. "Stay a moment, girl. There may be a reply. Is it from *Fabrik**?" It was the code-name for the factory housing the infantry battalion. "Yes?"

"Yessir."

"Good." He tore the envelope open eagerly. The message was brief but music to his ears. It read: "VB Grp. on its way. Already made good progress."

"Excellent," he said aloud and crumpling up the message he threw it in his wastepaper basket. He leaned back in his chair, feeling in an expansive mood, now that things were going so well. "How old are you, Heidi?" he asked.

She looked surprised at the question, and the fact that he knew her name. In a way she was a little flattered, especially as he called her by her first name instead of the usual *"Fraulein"* of the office. "Eighteen, *Reichsleiter*," she replied.

"A good age. An innocent age." He looked at her penetratingly. "You are innocent, Heidi, aren't you?"

She blushed and lowered her eyes. "Yes *Reichsleiter*," she whispered in a voice so low that he could barely hear her.

"Well, now that is a very good thing," he said, his voice suddenly thick and a little hoarse. "I'm afraid too many of our German women have been corrupted by this terrible war. They have thrown morality out of the window, I fear. Naturally I know you would make even *that* sacrifice for the Führer and the Fatherland if called upon to do so." He emphasized the "that", and he saw that she knew what he meant.

"I suppose so, sir, if I were called upon to do so," she answered in a little voice.

---

* *Fabrik* is the German word for "factory".

Bormann rose to his feet and gave her a fake smile, hoping the bulge in his breeches was not already showing. "I think you are a very brave staying here with the Führer, but I insist that you leave as soon as it's dark. Your life is too precious to be sacrificed at the eleventh hour. You are Germany's future, my dear." Again he gave her the fake smile. "But it still not yet dark. You can spend some time with me, can't you, dear?"

"Why yes, *Herr Reichsleiter*," she stuttered, a little puzzled. "Anything you say, sir."

"Good, good." He reached across and touched her thin, pale cheek. "You need something to put a little colour in those cheeks of yours, something to cheer you up on this sad day." He turned and opened the little icebox next to the closet. "I have a cool bottle of champus here. Will you not share a little with me, Heidi?"

She blushed again. "I've never drunk champagne before, sir. They say it gets up your nose – the bubbles that is – and makes you sneeze."

Bormann laughed. "Do they now? Well, we'll see." He took out the bottle, uncorked and poured her a generous portion into an enamel mug. Personally he would have preferred schnapps, but he had always found that champagne, for some reason, got into a woman's bloodstream quicker than hard booze and made them tipsier – and sexier – sooner. He handed her the mug and poured a mug for himself. "*Prosit, Fraulein Heidi,*" he said, raising his glass. "That you may have a long and happy life – and many children." He laughed.

She did, too, though a litte hesitantly, then raised her mug and took a careful sip. "Oh it tastes nice and sweet," she exclaimed with childlike simplicity.

"Then drink it all up, that's a good girl," Bormann encouraged her, already savouring the thought of undressing her and taking her virginal, skinny body. It was an age since he had last taken a virgin. "There's plenty more in the bottle."

"Should I, sir?"

"Of course, you should, dear," he said with faked enthusiasm. "Do you the world of good. Cheer up anyone, champagne will. Look at me with all my responsibilities. Champus cheers me up." He poured her another mugful.

On the third mug she was giggling all the time, her thin cheeks flushed, as he told her the story of how the Führer had always believed he was a vegetarian, too, until Hitler had caught him redhanded cutting off a huge chunk of salami. Thereafter the Führer had always called him privately "my dear sausage-vegetarian".

"Oh, I say, *Herr Reichsleiter*, is that what the Führer said to *you*?"

"No matter, I am not a proud man, just one of the many," he said winningly. "Now then my dear, why don't we get to know each other a little more? You can call me Martin if you wish and I say, why don't you just come over here?"

"But there is no seat," she objected tipsily.

"Oh yes there is," he chided. "On my lap."

"*Reichsleiter* – I mean, Martin. Would you allow that?"

"Naturally, I'd be delighted. Come on now, don't hesitate. I'm beginning to like you a great deal."

Once more she giggled and then hesitantly she came round the desk and carefully sat herself down on Bormann's lap, which was very unwise for he had something hard and penetrating waiting for her there. She looked at him, shocked in a kind of drunken way. "Don't worry, little Heidi," he reassured her as his big paw parted her skinny knees and started to slide up her thigh, "I shall take care of you. You have nothing to fear . . ."

# TWO

Schulze saw the Russian in the same instant that the Russian saw him. He tore the pin from the stick grenade, flung it and dropped to the cobbles, crying frantically, "Hit the dirt, lads!"

"Twenty . . . twenty-two . . . twenty-four . . ." Schulze counted off the seconds feverishly.

The grenade exploded in a vivid, angry flash. Red-hot, razor-sharp splinters of steel hissed through the air. Schulze's head felt as if it must burst out of his helmet. The blast hit his face like a slap from a damp, flabby fist. Automatically he opened his mouth to prevent his eardrums from bursting. In that same instant the Russian was tossed high. When he hit the littered cobbles again, he was minus both arms. They lay on the ground like blood-red branches. But there were more Russians behind him.

"Return their fire!" Kuehn yelled frantically.

The sudden appearance of what seemed to be a Russian assault troop had caught the Battle Group by surprise. The infantry at the factory had assured them that there were no Russians between them and the Führerbunker. But there were, and now lying in the gutters and crouching in the doorways of the ruined houses, the Wotan men and those of the other SS units who had survived the trek here, returned the enemy fire.

Schulze, out at point, and cut off by the Russians who

had infiltrated to his rear, knew instinctively he was in trouble. To his immediate front there were at least a dozen Russians firing at him and he had a sneaking suspicion there were others attempting to outflank him. Snapping off single shots to the left and right just to keep the Russians' heads down, for he was attempting to conserve his ammunition, his mind raced as he considered his position. He knew sooner or later his comrades of Wotan would attempt to reach him; they never abandoned a comrade in SS Assault Regiment Wotan. But he didn't want that. Some of the Wotan troopers would be killed or wounded in the attempt. He had to get out of the mess by himself and before the others made their rescue attempt.

To his rear, Lieutenant Kuehn shouted angrily, "Keep yourselves down and keep on firing! Do you hear that, Corporal Matz?"

Schulze knew what that meant. Matzi was already attempting to get the rescue operation underway. He'd better do something – *quick*. He caught his breath. Two Russians, Siberians by the look of them, small men with yellow Mongolian faces, were running straight at him, bayonets levelled. "Well, I'll piss in my boot!" he exclaimed. "They ain't got all their cups in their cupboard." He raised the Schmeisser and aimed at the running figures. He pressed the trigger. Nothing happened. "Shit on the shingle," he cursed angrily. His magazine was empty.

Now they were almost on him, yelling crazily, sweat streaming down their oval faces. Hastily Schulze rose to his feet, holding the Schmeisser by the muzzle like a bat. The first Siberian lunged at him. Schulze parried the thrust easily. With all his strength he whacked the butt of the machine pistol against the Siberian's face. Blood spurted from his nose and ears and he slammed against the nearest wall, sliding down it slowly, unconscious before he hit the ground.

Schulze grabbed his bayonetted rifle, and faced up to the second Siberian. Just in time he parried the Russian's thrust. Blades clashed. Schulze lunged forward. The other man was quicker. He dodged to one side. He swung his rifle and thrust at Schulze with the brass-shod butt.

Schulze turned his head just in time. The Siberian's rifle caught him a tremendous blow on the shoulder. Another man would have reeled back under such an impact. Not Schulze. He yelped with pain but did not budge. He knew he was done for once he hit the ground. Instead he lunged forward. His bayonet connected with something hard. The Russian howled. His rifle fell from suddenly nerveless fingers. Schulze's bayonet had severed the tendons of his right wrist. Schulze grinned hugely, but the Siberian wasn't finished yet.

The Siberian thrust his boot into Schulze's guts, as if he were a dancer doing a high kick. In the same instant, he grabbed the German's tunic with his good hand and pulled him down on top of himself. Suddenly Schulze's nostrils were assailed by a heavy pungent odour, a compound of sweat, garlic, black Russian tobacco and some kind of scent or cologne. The smell puzzled him and it took him seconds to realise that the Siberian was fumbling for something inside his pocket.

Schulze tried to grab the man's hand, but failed. Something gleamed in the ruddy light cast by the fires everywhere. Schulze gasped. It was a cut-throat razor! The hairs at the back of Schulze's broad head stood up in fear. His big left hand shot out and this time successfully grabbed the Siberian's fist. With his other, two fingers extended stiffly, he thrust home into the man's nostrils. Schulze didn't hesitate. He ripped the wet cavities upwards.

The Siberian's scream of sheer agony was drowned in the sudden flood of hot blood which threatened to choke him. The cut-throat razor dropped with a clatter to the cobbles. Schulze grabbed it. He exerted more pressure, forcing the Siberian's head backwards so that his throat was exposed. Schulze grunted. With all his strength he slashed the sharp blade across the man's throat just above the adam's apple, while the Siberian writhed and struggled helplessly. *Once, twice, three* times – viciously with his breath coming in great hectic sobs. Suddenly the Siberian went limp. He was dead. Schulze pulled his fingers out of the dead man's nose and dropped the razor. He lay there next to his victim, seemingly helpless, too exhausted to do anything, hating the dead Russian bitterly for having made him do this terrible thing.

Matz sized up the situation immediately. He saw that Schulze was temporarily at the end of his tether, and that in a matter of moments the Russians would be attacking again from the big ruined house in which they were lodged to the right. Schulze, if he didn't move, would be their first victim. "Frig that for a game o' soldiers," he cried at no one in particular. "Bazooka man," he called to the young Wotan trooper sheltering a little way behind him as the Russian bullets whined and howled off the brickwork all about them. "Gimme that popgun of yours."

Obediently the young trooper handed him the rocket-launch with its bulbous, vaselike head.

"What are you going to do, Corporal?" Kuehn asked sharply.

Matz didn't answer. He hadn't time to do so. Instead he hobbled out into the centre of the burning street, ignoring the bullets cutting the air all around. Carefully he balanced the long tubelike weapon in his shoulder and pulled the trigger. A long streak of angry scarlet flame flew from one end, as the projectile streaked towards the Russian-held house.

The projectile slammed into the wall. The whole house trembled. A Russian plunged to his death from an upper window as a great hole appeared in the wall and then Matz was limping forward, bazooka thrown away, spraying the house with slugs from his Schmeisser.

As one, the Wotan troopers rose from their cover. Whooping and howling like drunken Red Indians on the warpath, they streamed behind Matz, who had stood at the door of the Russian-held building spraying the interior with bullets before disappearing inside. Moments later the Wotan troopers were in after him.

Now the little battle for the house developed into a bloody, bitter series of hand-to-hand fights between individual soldiers, swaying back and forth in rooms, on the stairs, in the yard outside. Neither side gave or expected quarter in this desperate close-combat fighting. When a soldier went down, his opponent rained blow after blow at his unprotected face until it turned into a horrifying red pulp. Rifles were abandoned in these close quarters for anything – bayonet, knife, entrenching tool – with which the crazed, frenzied men could hack, gouge, chop, slash, slice. Overcome by an animal bloodlust, German and Russian fought savagely by grunting and gasping, frantic, unintelligible cries coming from their open, gasping mouths.

Then it was all over as abruptly as it had started. Men lay moaning on the ground among the dead, Russian and German, while the surviving Russians raised their hands nervously, eyeing the wild, excited, sweat-lathered faces of the victors, as if trying to find some spark of pity there. But there was none. Curtly Kuehn ordered, as if it was the most obvious thing in the world, "We have no time for prisoners – shoot them!"

The men looked at each other. This was the worst possible time to start shooting Red Army prisoners, now that Berlin was just about captured. All of them knew that. So did Schulze. He rose to his feet and just as Kuehn raised his pistol and was about to start firing, his big paw came down and knocked the pistol to one side. "None of that, Lieutenant Kuehn," he bellowed, face hard and threatening.

Kuehn spun round, his steel-blue eyes blazing. "How dare you?" he snorted. "What kind of piggery is this where an NCO strikes an officer?"

"I didn't strike you," Schulze said calmly, standing his ground. "I just made you lower your pistol. This is the wrong time to shoot the Ivans. We might be prisoners ourselves by nightfall. What then?"

"We won't, I can tell you that," Kuehn retorted, spittle running down the sides of his mouth with rage.

"Let 'em go. Hey you, soldier boy" – he turned to a Wotan trooper – "give 'em a kick in the arse and tell 'em to bugger off home to Russia."

"*Davoi . . . davoi*," the trooper shouted – like all the Wotan "old hares", he had picked up pidgin Russian during the years Wotan had spent on the Eastern Front. "*Za Russiya . . . davoi . . .*"

For a moment nothing happened. The prisoners couldn't believe that they were not going to be shot. Then they realised they were being released. Several of them went down on their knees. Others grabbed the surprised trooper's hand and kissed it, then all of them were running away into the maze of ruined, smoking houses. A few moments later they had disappeared altogether.

Kuehn watched with the rest till they had gone before

turning to Schulze. Harshly he said, "You've made yourself a bad enemy this day, Sergeant. Do anything like that once more and you're a dead man."

With that he was gone, leaving Schulze to tell himself that Kuehn's threat was no idle one. He meant it all right.

# THREE

"This then is the last time," Hitler said a little sadly and pressed his secretary's hand. She could not answer. Her eyes were filled with tears. One by one the Führer shook the hands of those who had served so faithfully through the long years of war. Slowly he then followed Eva, his new wife, back into their private apartments and closed the door firmly behind him. It was three o'clock on the afternoon of April 30th.

Outside they waited tensely for that to happen which would have to happen. The minutes ticked by. The only sound now was their tense breathing and that of the artillery fire from outside which filtered into the bunker.

Inside his anteroom Hitler toyed with his Walther. A second lay on the red carpet. On the sofa behind the table at which he sat, Eva Braun lay slumped – dead. She had taken poison. Before him on the console there was a picture of his mother as a young woman – nothing else. Slowly, very slowly, he opened his mouth and brought up the pistol. He inserted the muzzle into his mouth. His nose wrinkled a little at the taste of gun oil. His knuckle whitened on the trigger. It was nearly all over now. He took final pressure. The gun went off. His world exploded in a flurry of red, violent light. Then hc was dead. It was three-thirty on Monday April 30th, 1945. The greatest tyrant the world had ever known was dead.

In the conference room, Bormann, Linge and Guensche heard the single shot. They hesitated for a moment, then they broke into the anteroom. Hitler lay sprawled face down over the table. As he had fallen, he had knocked over a flower vase and spilled the water over Eva's black dress.

Unnerved by what he had just seen, Guensche, the giant adjutant, staggered back into the conference room where he met the chauffeur Kempka. "For God's sake," the latter cried, "what's going on? You must be crazy to send men to almost certain death just for two hundred litres of petrol."

The SS officer looked down at him, his face ashen. "The Chief is dead," he said in a broken voice.

"How?"

Guensche couldn't bring himself to say the dreaded words. Instead he pointed his forefinger like the barrel of a pistol and put it to his mouth.

Kempka gasped. "And where's Eva?" he stuttered.

Finally Guensche found his voice once more. "She's with him," he said weakly in the same instant that Linge and Hitler's doctor came out bearing the body of their master, covered in a blanket. Behind them came Bormann, carrying Eva, her blonde hair hanging down loose.

The sight of Eva in Bormann's arms, a man she had always hated, was too much for her chauffeur. "Not one more step," he barked threateningly. "I'll carry Eva."

Wordlessly Bormann handed her over. Kempka followed up the stairs after the others so he didn't see the sudden smile of happiness on Bormann's face as he told himself he was free at last. He could go.

Outside the Russian shelling had commenced yet again.

Plumes of dark smoke, tinged with flame, rose everywhere. Buildings shook and collapsed. But Kempka had no eyes for the artillery bombardment. He saw Hitler sprawled on the ground five metres away. It was in a small depression next to a cement mixer. Hitler's trousers were pulled up, with the right foot turned slightly inwards. Kempka smiled a little sadly as he lowered Eva's still warm body next to Hitler's. It was the characteristic position which Hitler had always adopted when he had driven him on long car journeys.

Shells started to slam home next to the ruined Chancellery. The SS men ducked for cover as shrapnel hissed alarmingly through the air. There they crouched for a few minutes until the Russian gunners turned their attention on other targets. Now they emerged hastily from their cover and picked up the jerricans.

Shaking with self-loathing for doing this, and revulsion, Kempka helped them to begin sprinkling petrol over the corpses. He thought, I can't do it, but I am doing it. He saw the same reaction in the faces of Linge and Guensche.

Can after can of petrol were now emptied into the depression where the two bodies lay until it was filled with fuel. Then, pausing to take a breath of fresh air away from the cloying stench of petrol, Guensche said, "We can ignite it by chucking in a grenade."

Kempka shook his head. "No, we couldn't do that," he said firmly. "We can't mutilate Eva, she was so beautiful, and the Chief. Here, look at that big rug." Somehow a rug had been placed in the ruined garden. "We can set it alight and use the rug to ignite the petrol."

"Good idea," the Adjutant cried above the noise of the shelling. "Here. The matches!" He tossed the box to Kempka who had doused the rug in petrol. Carefully the chauffeur applied a lighted match to one end of the rug. It started to burn fiercely, immediately.

Hurriedly he snatched it up and ran with it to the bodies. He tossed it into the depression and stepped back hastily. Just in time. The petrol went up in flames with an angry whoosh. A red-hot ball of fire shot upwards. The sudden heat was terrific. Kempka put his hands up to shield his face, then staggered back to a safer distance, where, together with the other two, he watched in horrified fascination as the greedy flames began to consume the bodies . . .

Bormann was making his last preparations. As soon as the van de Brug Battle Group reported in, he would have them fed. Then he would hand the Dutchman the first half of the thousand dollars to do with as he wished. Then they would set off that same night for the Havel. He reasoned they would stand a better chance during the hours of darkness when the Russian shelling would have to stop.

Well satisfied with himself, Bormann began to strip. Now he would change into the SS major-general's uniform. He'd arm himself too – just in case. He had a machine pistol and his duty pistol in the closet. As he stripped to his underwear, he thought of Heidi the previous evening and licked his thick lips at the memory. She had just loved it despite the pain.

Screaming and biting she had writhed back and forth frighteningly, as he had shoved it into her lithe young body, her lips a gleaming scarlet as she mouthed the most foul obscenities, learned God knows where. Then she had arched her spine, stopping in the middle of the wild frantic movement, digging her nails painfully into his buttocks as she had done so, and had shrieked through gritted teeth, "*Oh shit . . . shit . . . shit!*"

97

And it hadn't stopped there. Afterwards she had done things to him which completely flabbergasted him when he thought she had been a virgin only a couple of hours before. Indeed she had taken to sex like a duck to water. For a moment or two he was inclined to ask her to come with him, but then he realised that she'd only be a nuisance. Besides, there would be women and girls enough where he was going. Naturally he would not have his ready-made harem of the typing pool. But he had the wherewithal to purchase as many women as he wanted. He tapped the gems, now safely tucked away in the inside pocket of the general's tunic.

He buttoned up the tunic and looked at himself in the mirror. His chest was devoid of decorations, save the War Service Cross, Third Class, and the Blood Order which Hitler had given him for the months he had spent in jail on a murder charge in the old days of the Party. Still he told himself he looked imposing enough, giving off an air of natural authority; he'd play the role of an SS general quite well, he thought.

He buckled on his pistol belt, tapped the tunic to reassure himself that his precious gems and dollars were safely stowed away and decided to go out into the corridor for a last look around.

Outside the party mood had mostly vanished. Now that Hitler was dead an oppressive doomsday atmosphere had settled on the bunker, as the officials and officers stood in little groups debating what to do next. Those who would escape were already looking constantly at their watches, as they waited for night to fall. The others who were to remain behind, not wanting to take the risk, sat or lounged, staring into space, occasionally breaking off to drink from the bottles that were everywhere.

Magda Goebbels, the wife of the Minister of Propaganda, passed by him in a kind of trance. He had always fancied her. She was blonde and busty, much too pretty for the ugly little Minister with the ugly face, uglier body and his poisonous tongue. "What will you do, Magda?" he asked as she passed.

She shook her head, tears in her eyes. "All is lost," she said hopelessly. "I shall poison the children myself."

Even Bormann was shocked at that – she had five beautiful blonde children – and she was going to kill them by poison. Although he was abandoning his own six children, safe in the Austrian Alps, he could never have brought himself to do away with them. "You can't do that," he said.

But Magda was no longer listening as she hurried away, carrying the poison pills for her unsuspecting children in her hand.

Bormann shrugged and walked over to where Heidi, dark circles under her eyes, was still working at her machine. "Any news of the Battle Group?" he asked eagerly.

"Yes, *Herr Reichsleiter*," she said looking up. "They signalled back to *Fabrik* that they had been held up by Russians in the *Tiergarten*. *Fabrik* has signalled to us that van de Brug hopes to have cleared a way through by the time it's dark."

"Thank you, Heidi," he said and forced a smile. The *Tiergarten* was less than a kilometre away. All was going well.

Heidi put a finger in her mouth and started to suck it like a little child. But Bormann, his pulse quickening, knew that this was no little girl act. The little minx was offering him something else. He licked his lips. Should he? Should he take up her offer?

The single shot from Goebbels' apartments awoke him to reality. The Minister of Propaganda had obviously just shot himself. In a minute they'd break in and find him, his wife and the five children all dead. No, there was no time for sexual dalliances now. There'd be time enough for that in the weeks to come. First he had to escape.

Suddenly on impulse he reached in his tunic and brought out fifty dollars. He gave her the note, saying, "This is an American fifty dollar bill. Now it is worth a small fortune. Take it and join one of the groups leaving after dark. It will buy you many things, even safety."

She pouted but accepted the note. Slowly she removed the wet finger from between her scarlet lips and looked at it knowingly. *"Danke, Herr Reichsleiter,"* she said slyly. "What have I done to deserve it? How can I make it up to you, sir?" Again she looked at the wet, gleaming finger. He fled . . .

# FOUR

"There is no doubt about it," the drunken *kreisleiter** in his dirty, rumpled brown uniform was saying, "once the relieving army reaches Berlin, the Führer will immediately employ the latest secret weapons." He placed his pudgy hand on van de Brug's knee winningly. "The situation will change dramatically. The Tommies and the *Amis* will join in with us as allies and together we'll march against the Ivans. By June, perhaps August at the latest, we will have won the war." He tapped the side of his big nose and winked knowingly. "I have friends in high places. I know of what I speak." He took another hefty slug from the flatman he had been carrying when the Battle Group had bumped into him and his party in the confusion of a smoke-shrouded *Tiergarten* with red, white and green tracer zipping back and forth in a lethal morse.

"I see," van de Brug said coldly. "I see, *Kreisleiter*," he said without enthusiasm. "Let us pray that the relief army gets here quickly or there won't be anything to relieve."

The *kreisleiter* belched and apologized and then said, "Never fear, young man, the Führer in his infinite wisdom is simply biding his time. Everything is arranged, determined, planned to the very last dot above the 'i'."

Van de Brug sniffed.

* Party County Leader.

The *kreisleiter* took another swig of his firewater. "You are young and young men tend to be sceptical."

"I'm paid to fight, not be to be sceptical or anything else."

The *kreisleiter* didn't seem to hear. He said expansively, "Belief is the basis of success in combat, my dear fellow." He fingered his Iron Cross, Third Class, from the old war and added, "We did in the trenches. That's how we stuck it out so long. It is essential that if the nation is to believe in final victory despite what is happening in the pres—" He stopped short.

There was an obscene howl, followed by a spine-chilling bansheelike howling. Great trails of black smoke streaked into the burning afternoon sky. "Stalin organs!" the *kreisleiter* yelled above the shriek. He dropped his flat-man and scuttled down into a ditch, as if the Devil himself was after him, as the shells from the Russian multiple mortars slammed into the park with such an impact that the very ground trembled. "Victory in June '45, *Kreisleiter*!" van de Brug shouted after him maliciously.

Schulze came crawling up, panting, face lathered in sweat and dirt. He dropped into the ditch next to the Dutch officer as a vicious burst of machine-gun fire sliced the air just where his head had been only a few moments before. "Jesus H, Christ," he cursed angrily, "that nearly had my frigging turnip." He meant his head.

"Report!" van de Brug snapped, ignoring the remark, as he indeed seemed to ignore all the mayhem and frightened confusion all about him. For the whole horizon above the city was ablaze. Dozens of fires raged. Great mushrooms of black smoke ascended to the heavens on all sides. Whistles shrilled. Men and women, laden with rucksacks, ran for cover. It seemed like the end of the world, but van de Brug remained calm and efficient as if this was a perfectly normal state for humanity to be in.

"They've got snipers out everywhere," Schulze gasped, indicating his helmet. There was a neat, curled hole in it. "Nearly got my ticket on that one."

"What else? Snipers can be dealt with," van de Brug snapped.

Schulze hesitated. He knew that the Dutchman and Kuehn were up to something, but he felt that van de Brug was a more reasonable man than the sadistic American. "Well, sir, don't you think we should turn back while we've got time still?" He ducked as a vicious burst of machine-gun fire skimmed the length of the ditch. "I don't think we've got much of a future if we go much further. It'll be a one-way trip – and to what purpose? Germany's finished. Everybody knows that." He stopped short, feeling he had said enough already.

Van de Brug studied his broad, dirty face for a moment, quite camly and without anger. "If anyone else had heard such treasonable remarks, *Oberscharführer*, they would have had you shot out of hand, decorated hero that you are." He indicated Schulze's broad, bemedalled chest. "That doesn't concern me, however. All I'm concerned with is carrying out my orders. I've been ordered to the bunker and that is what I shall do." He paused and looked hard at the big NCO with his one good eye. "Besides, Schulze, you never know, there might be a little something in it for us all, if we play our cards right." Then he snapped, businesslike again, "All right, Sergeant, take half a dozen men and sort out those snipers at the double. We can't hang around this place much longer."

"Yessir," Schulze answered and scurried away down the ditch to find Matz and the others, wondering as he did so what the Dutchman's last statement had really meant; what that "little something" really was . . .

Now they had moved out of the Park, leaving three of their number stretched out in the scorched grass, shot by the Russian snipers before they had shot them out of the trees to which they had tied themselves. The streets were filled with panic-stricken civilians and a good number of soldiers too, probably deserters trying to sneak out of the city before it was too late. Desperately the Battle Group fought its way through the crazed confusion all around them, trying to ignore the screams of the people trapped in the blazing ruins to either side of the streets. Charred, shrunken corpses lay in the gutters. Bodies hung from skeletal trees like weird human fruit. A maddened horse clattered down the centre of the street, its mane and tail on fire, followed by a crazed, howling dachshund.

A gas main exploded to their right. Like a gigantic blowtorch its searing flame shot house-high into the sky. Covering their nostrils and mouths with handkerchieves against the stink of singed hair and charred flesh, they passed a group of sweating, filthy soldiers sorting out the bodies of dead children. Hysterically weeping and howling women, wringing their hands in utter despair, watched as the dead children were swung into the waiting truck like logs of wood.

But darkness was beginning to fall. Still that lunar landscape remained revealed in all its stark awesome frightfulness. Once magnificent trees, stripped of their foliage by the ceaseless artillery fire, looking not unlike outsize toothpicks. Jagged heaps of brick rubble and grotesquely twisted steel rods and tubes which had once been fine houses. Abandoned trucks, some with their drivers slumped dead at the wheels. A burnt-out tram. Inside were a row of charred skeletons, burnt alive, helmets still on their grinning skulls. A boot with the leg still in it. Horror after horror . . .

But as the darkness started to fall, the gunfire began to diminish. Schulze wiped the sweat from his forehead and gasped to Matz who crouched next him as they edged their way down the Königsplatz on the lookout for enemy snipers. "Thank Christ for that, Matzi. Those frigging guns could drive a feller absolutely *meschugge*."

"You're nuts already," Matz commented drily. "We're all nuts going along with those two foreigners. What an absolute heap of shit!"

"But what can we do?" Schulze objected. "If those two officers don't get us for doing a bunk, some sod of a chained dog," he meant a military policeman, "would, and string us up on the nearest tree in null, comma, zero seconds."

"I suppose you're right," Matz said gloomily. "But we've got to do something. Corporal Matz ain't got no intention of dying *now* for frigging Fatherland, Folk and Führer."

A little while later, while they were sheltering from enemy machine-gun fire in a cellar, packed with frightened civilians huddled around a pear-shaped "People's Radio", Matz and the rest learned that there would now be no need to die for the last of the trilogy. The lively foxtrot which was coming from it was interrupted abruptly. "This is Radio Hamburg," a solemn voice announced. "We interrupt our programme to bring you a grave and solemn announcement. Please stand by." The voice vanished and there was snatch of *Tannhäuser* by Wagner before the solemn voice came back to say, "Our Führer, Adolf Hitler, fighting to the last breath against Bolshevism, fell for Germany this afternoon in his operation headquarters in the Reich Chancellery. This day

Grand Admiral Doenitz, the Führer's successor, will now speak to the German people . . ."

Most of those in the cellar were no longer listening. Some women cried softly. The older civilians looked grave. A wizened old worker in a leather jacket actually smiled. But all of them, whether they had been for or against Hitler, looked shocked. Hitler had been part of their lives for so long that they could not visualize a time without him.

Schulze looked at Matz in the suddenly silent cellar, the only sound the soft weeping of the women and the chatter of the machine guns outside. His eyes posed the unspoken question. *What now?*

Matz nodded his understanding.

Slowly, very slowly, as if it took a great deal of effort to do so, Schulze turned his gaze on the two foreign officers. They, of all the people in the cellar, seemed strangely unaffected. Indeed the only emotion that their faces revealed was impatience, as if they could not get to the Führerbunker quickly enough. Why? he asked himself. What purpose could their daring and highly dangerous venture have now? Hitler was dead and with him the Third Reich. Automatically they were absolved from their personal oath of loyalty which every German soldier had had to swear on the swastika flag to the Führer. It *was all damn well over*!

But his questions went answered. Ten minutes later they were on their way once more through the glowing night, the darkness stabbed time and time again by scarlet flashes and the lethal morse of streams of tracer bullets zipping back and forth.

They clambered through a rough-and-ready barricade made up of Berlin trams and wrecked trucks. It had been defended to the death by a group of teenage Hitler Youth kids, boys and girls. They were sprawled everywhere in the extravagent poses of those who had been done to death violently. In the glowing darkness they could see that the girls had been raped. Their skirts were thrown up and their white knickers pulled down to their ankles. Blood still trickled down the inside of their skinny little thighs.

Schulze breathed hard, but said nothing; he simply couldn't find the words.

They pushed on. The gunfire had now almost ceased. Berlin, what was left of it, was settling down for another long night of waiting for a dawn that might not come for many. And then there it was – the Reich Chancellery, a stark ruin set against lurid flames of the fires in the background. Van de Brug looked triumphantly at Kuehn and yelled above the machine gun fire, "We've done it, Kuehn . . . *we've done it!*"

# FIVE

"As far as the *Wehrmacht* is concerned," the fat doctor in the bloodstained apron was pontificating to the colonel with the purple stripe of the General Staff running down the side of his breeches, "syphilis means the loss of a fighting soldier for twenty-seven days and gonorrhoea for fifteen. Of course our field brothels are well organised but how can one ensure that the men use them, eh? Really, that's the problem. Of course, some men pick up the disease purposely so that one has to take them out of the line."

"Disgraceful!" the staff colonel snapped, eyes flashing behind his silver, schoolmaster's pince-nez. "These days everyone fiddles, scrounges, malingers, tricks, betrays, lines his own pockets. Germany is totally corrupted. One wonders what Germany is coming to." He sighed like a man whose patience was being sorely tried.

"Shoot more of them out of hand," the fat doctor said easily as Kuehn and van de Brug pushed by the couple moaning in the corridor of the Führerbunker. "That would make the others jump."

"Radical, but admirable," the staff colonel agreed. "More discipline is what we need, especially now that our beloved Führer is dead." He pulled a silver flask from his pocket and took a deep draught before handing the flask to the fat doctor. "Here, *Herr Doktor*," he gasped, "have a taste. It's the last of the Martell I brought back with me from France last year when we were forced to – er – withdraw."

Van de Brug looked at Kuehn and shrugged, his face full of contempt.

Kuehn nodded and then spoke in English, the language they both used when alone and far from prying ears, for security reasons. "They're nuts. All the Krauts are nuts," he rasped. "Don't they know the fucking war is lost? Piet, what kind of guys are these?"

"Al," van de Brug replied, "*Die Moppen*, as we call the Germans, have not been known for their closeness to reality. They live in a dream world of their own. No matter. That kind of crap suits our kind of purpose to a 't'."

"Yeah, Piet," Al Kuehn agreed. "Okay, let's find this guy Bormann. I guess he's our best bet for our purposes, now that old Adolf is dead."

"Of course he is, Al," van de Brug agreed enthusiastically. "He's our ticket to freedom – and a lot of money." He made the continental gesture of counting notes with his forefinger and thumb. "Bormann's our passport to the future." He grinned maliciously. "Though the poor sucker doesn't know it yet."

They found Bormann's office at the end of the yellow-lit corridor and knocked at the door. Bormann was expecting them. "Come in," he called eagerly and rose to his feet beind the desk.

They entered and saluted. But Bormann would have nothing of it. He pushed a bottle of schnapps in their direction and a tray of glasses. "Please feel at ease, gentlemen," he gushed. "There is no time for formalities now. Those days are over for good. I'm just an ordinary chap just like the two of you."

109

You're just full of piss and vinegar, van de Brug told himself, feeling nothing but contempt for the one-time so important party official, scared shitless, hoping we're going to get you out of the mess you've fallen into.

All the same, he and Kuehn accepted glasses of schnapps – they needed them after what they had been through. Together they raised their glasses at Bormann's command and drained them in the German fashion when he cried, "*Prost-ex!*"

"Now then," Bormann said expansively, a winning smile on his broad face, "first things first." He pulled out the five hundred dollars he had ready and gave them to van de Brug. "These are yours to do with what you wish. It's a small fortune in Europe today, I can tell you. There will be another five hundred for you and your command, once you have delivered me safely to the other side of the Havel. I hope that is satisfactory."

Van de Brug told himself the Party boss sounded like some Yid tailor delivering a new suit to a client. Carelessly, not even bothering to count it, he stowed the dollars in his inner pocket. "Not quite," he said deliberately.

Bormann's fake smile vanished. "Not quite? How do you mean?"

"We want something else, I and Lieutenant Kuehn."

"Something else?"

"Yes. Germany's finished. Once we've got you out, we're gonna do a dive and to do that we need passports – say Swiss, perhaps even Swedish." Van de Brug shrugged carelessly, but he did not take his eyes off Bormann's shifty face for an instant.

"Passports! But where should I obtain neutral passports for you at this late hour? Gentlemen, what you are asking is impossible."

Without asking permission Kuehn reached over and poured a glass of schnapps for van de Brug then for himself. He raised it to his lips and took a hefty drink of the fiery liquid. The gesture was not lost on Bormann. He was no longer in charge. They were. His shoulders bent a little in defeat, as he said, "All right, I'll do my best."

"Good," van de Brug snapped, very businesslike now. "Now we're not going out with any of the other escape parties. There are too many civilians and women in them. If we've got to fight the Ivans we don't want to be hampered by them. Is that clear?" he rasped.

"Yes, that is clear," Bormann replied with a newly found humility, as he realized just how much he was in the hands of the men opposite him.

"From what we've heard outside, there are six separate groups which are going to make an escape from the bunker this night. They are all going to use the same route." The Dutchman strode over to the map of Central Berlin pinned to the wall of Bormann's room. "Here's the bunker," he tapped the chart, "and here's the entrance to the nearest *U-Bahn* station." He meant Berlin's underground railway station. "They'll attempt to walk along the tracks until they come to the Friedrichstrasse railway station and there they will surface again, cross the Spree River – here – then head west or northwest until they can link up with the German forces in Northern Germany under Grand Admiral Doenitz."

Bormann nodded his understanding, but said nothing.

"Now we shall take the same route," van de Brug went on, "until we reach the Friedrichstrasse station. I think it is the safest way out of Central Berlin, then, however, we'll head for *Fabrik* . . ."

". . . the *Fabrik*?" Bormann interjected quickly.

"Yes." Van de Brug smiled coldly. "We have a truck

111

waiting for us there. With it we're going to make a dash down the Kaiserdamm for the Havel and those electric boats of yours."

"But," Bormann asked slowly, as if he were puzzled, "can a single truck carry the whole of the escort – those chaps of yours from Wotan?"

Van de Brug exchanged knowing looks with Kuehn and said in reply, "But who said we would be taking them with us all the way to the Havel, Herr Bormann?"

Bormann gave them a slow smile. He had always appreciated duplicity and double dealing. "So that's the way of it, eh?"

Van de Brug nodded. "That's the way of it, Herr Bormann," the Dutchman echoed his words . . .

Replete and belching at regular intervals, Matz and Schulze sat in the canteen, finishing off the rest of their thick green "fart soup", washing it down with generous droughts of cool Munich "suds". All around them there was hectic activity. Men and women preparing for the breakout, strapping heavy rucksacks to their backs, sticking pistols and grenades into their belts. Other simply drank and drank, as if they intended to drink themselves into oblivion. They were obviously the ones who wouldn't be going. They would wait for the Russians and whatever Fate decreed would happen to them then.

"What a crock o' shit this lot is!" Schulze said scornfully. "And it was them who sent us off to war. Five or six frigging years and all the lads from Wotan who got the chop. For what, eh?" He spat scornfully onto the floor.

"Yer," Matz agreed. "Now all they care about is saving their own precious hides. None of these shits are going to die for Folk, Fatherland and Führer if they can help it." He, too, spat on the floor to show his contempt.

"Hello, soldiers, aren't you going tonight?" It was a girl who didn't look a day over eighteen. She was pretty drunk, a stupid smile on her pretty little face and her blouse was open daringly to reveal her neat little breasts; when she bent and took a sip of Matz's beer without asking, he could see the pink-tipped nipples.

At any other time Matz would have been delighted, but not now. "Now, now, *Fraulein*," he chided her mildly as she staggered drunkenly and abruptly sat down on his lap. "You can't do that. You'd better pull yourself together and find a group to go with before . . ."

She gave him a wet kiss and said thickly, "You don't love me?" She flung her arms around his neck passionately.

"Get off!" Matz snorted and freed himself swiftly while Schulze guffawed and said, "You'll have to make an honest woman of her now, Matzi, old house. She's fallen in love with you – instantly."

The remark caused her to turn, swaying alarmingly as she did so. She blinked hard as if she were having difficulty in focusing her eyes. "Would you like to give me a kiss, Sergeant?"

"At any other time, *Fraulein*, I'd be honoured," Schulze said with great gallantry. "But the world's coming to an end and I'm in a hurry to jump off before it stops moving."

Again she swayed frighteningly and reached out for Matz's beer glass. He pulled it away from her in time, saying, "Now you've had enough, Miss. You'll never get out in this state."

"Your officers are drinking with *Reichsleiter* Bormann – the lecherous swine – and they're getting out . . . in a truck." She hiccuped and Matz had to catch her to prevent her from falling.

Matz and Schulze looked at her as one, worn, unshaven

faces suddenly very alert. "Did you say 'truck'?" Schulze barked.

"Yes." She nodded her head a little stupidly.

"How did you find that out?" Schulze asked.

"Because I was listening at the door. I think it's going to be a little one because your officer says you're not going with it." She giggled.

"It's the one they put under guard at the *Fabrik*," Matz said hurriedly.

"You're right," Schulze flashed back. He looked at the girl. "Little lady, we're taking you with us. Somehow – I don't know quite how yet – I think you've saved our bacon." He rose to his feet. "Take her, Matzi, over there into the shower room. Give her a shower and see if you can sober her up. And no funny business," he said threateningly, doubling his mighty fist, "or it'll be a knuckle sandwich if you do. I'm off to see if I can find her something to put on."

Heidi got off Matz's knee, giggling, silly and suddenly very happy. "Love to go under the shower with you, Corporal. Let's hurry." She swayed off.

Matz raised his eyes to the ceiling as if imploring some god on high to give him strength and patience and then he limped hurriedly after her.

Schulze grinned as they went, telling himself Matz would be happy enough if he managed to get a little finger, at least, under the shower, then he, too, turned and set off to find what he thought he'd need for the girl . . .

# SIX

Heidi giggled naughtily. "Are you going to stick it in me now?" she asked hopefully.

She had refused to undress herself, so Matz had done it for her. Now she stood under the shower brazenly, exposing her little breasts and the dark smudge of hair at the base of her stomach.

"No I'm not," Matz answered a little angrily. He would have dearly loved to have "stuck" it into her, but there wasn't time and he had to get the randy little bitch sober. "I'm going to give you a shower."

She giggled with delight. "Are you coming to join me?" she simpered.

"No I'm not. I've got a wooden leg."

"I don't mind. Take it off as well. I do love men's things, all hairy and dangling."

Matz had had enough. He turned on the tap of the shower and let the silly little girl have the full blast of the shower.

She sobbed and gasped, dancing on the dais as the full impact of the water hit her naked body. "It's cold, *shitting cold*!" she shrieked, her little breasts giggling up and down as she danced from one foot to the other, teeth suddenly chattering.

"I know it's frigging cold. It's supposed to be – to simmer you down and get your mind off male tails and onto the other things of life.2 He turned the tap up full pressure and the water shot down in an icy stream until she cried, "Enough . . . enough! . . . I'm all right now. I'll behave myself. But please, *please*, turn it off. I'm turning blue with cold."

Matz took pity on her. She was only a kid, even if she was a randy one. He turned off the tap, handed her a towel and as she began to pat herself with it, took another one and started drying her back. He knew time was of the essence. He had to help her to get dry quickly.

It was just then that Schulze strode through the door, holding an army private's uniform over his big arm. "Freeze those mitts, Matzi," he commanded sternly, "I'm not having any of that kind of piggery with the Miss."

"Just wiping her back, that's all," Matz replied.

"Yer, and what's that sticking out of yer breeches eh?"

"My mind is pure," Matz said. "How can I help what the rest of me does? It's human nature."

"Well, keep yer frigging human nature to itself and try not to stick it in nice little girls." He beamed at Heidi. "Here, put these togs on. They'll about fit yer." Then he added, "Oh, and put some of that cream on yer face." He put the little tin on the chair next to the uniform. "It's camouflage cream. Your boss, that feller Bormann, perhaps won't recognize you then."

Heidi had sobered up somewhat by now. Her tone was more serious and she looked from one "old hare" to the other and said in a sweet little voice, "Thank you for looking after me like this. I've been a bit of a fool, haven't I? I think it's this awful place."

"Don't worry," Schulze said, "We'll get you to safety. In thirty minutes we'll be out of this dump and then it'll be home to mother. Come on now, get dressed." He shot Matz a threatening look, as he stood there prepared to watch the naked girl put on her things. "Come on arse-with-ears," he growled. "She can put her knickers on without your help."

Kempka's group went first. It was made up of about thirty people, soldiers and civilians, some of them women but all of them were armed with machine pistols and hand grenades. For they knew they could expect little mercy from the enemy if they ran into the Russians. Van de Brug watched them go, emerging into the chaos of a shattered, burning Berlin, then he turned to Bormann. "Stick close to me. Keep your eyes on me all the time and do exactly as I do. Is that understood?"

Despite the fact he was dressed as a major-general, Bormann answered dutifully, as if he were a humble private. "*Jawohl, Sturmbannführer.*"

Van de Brug said "Good." Then he turned to Kuehn and said in English, which he was confident that no one else in the group understood, "Watch him at all times, Al, till we get out of this mess. Remember what he means for us."

Kuehn grinned evilly. "You betcha, Piet." He slapped his pistol. "Nobody's coming between me and the loot."

Listening to them speaking English, but not understanding a word of what they were saying, Schulze frowned. But he could guess they were up to no good. But thanks to the little teleprinter operator, Heidi, who was now being quietly sick in the corner of the corridor, they did know that the two officers were going to ditch them once they got that truck at the *Fabrik*. His big broad face hardened. "That's what you think, shitehawks," he told himself grimly. "But you've got to get up early in the morning to catch Mrs Schulze's handsome son with his knickers down."

117

"Stand by everybody!" van de Brug's harsh voice cut into his thoughts. He glanced down at the green glowing dial of his wristwatch. "We're going up in exactly two minutes. I, with *Reichsleiter* Bormann, will lead. Lieutenant Kuehn will command the main body. You, Sergeant Schulze and Corporal Matz, will bring up the rear. Don't bunch. Don't fire unless fired upon." His one eye stared hard at the line of tense, worried faces in the poor yellow light of the single naked bulb in that part of the corridor. "If anybody's hit it's just tough titty for the one concerned. We're not stopping for any wounded. The wounded man stays where he lays. Clear?"

"Clear," the mumble of agreement came back reluctantly. For Wotan had never abandoned its casualties. In Russia, rather than let their seriously wounded fall into the hands of the Ivans, they shot the poor unfortunates themselves.

Heidi, who had finished being sick, looked worried at the words, but Schulze pressed her skinny little hand hastily and said with surprising tenderness for him, "Don't take any notice of him. Me and Matz, crippled peg-leg as he is, will look after you. Never fear."

Now van de Brug, one eye fixed on his wristwatch started to count off the remaining seconds. "*Sixty . . . forty seconds . . . twenty . . . ten seconds, nine . . . eight . . . seven . . . six . . . five . . . four . . . three . . . two . . . one . . . LOS!*"

He grabbed the first rung of the iron ladder attached to the concrete wall effortlessly. Next moment he was climbing upwards towards the surface. Bormann followed a little more slowly, puffing with the unusual exertion.

Kuehn watched his polished boots disappear through the opening, then he snapped, "Follow me. At the double now." He grabbed the first stanchion and started to climb

118

rapidly. Schulze pushed the frightened little girl between himself and Matz. "Now remember that's where you stay, Miss, till we're finished with this business. Between me and Matz. All right, *los*."

Awkwardly the little Corporal levered his wooden leg on the bottom rung of the ladder and started to pull himself, followed an instant later by the girl. Then came Sergeant Schulze carrying his machine pistol in his big right paw as if it was a child's popgun. Matz popped his head through the opening, glad of a breath of fresh air after the fetid, fume-laden atmosphere of the bunker.

The whole of central Berlin was in flames. The sky burned a fierce red. To their immediate front in the Chancellery garden two pale flames flickered and burnt. Matz heard Bormann say, "The Führer and his new bride Eva." His voice was toneless and without emotion.

"New bride," Matz mused and pursed his lips. "Didn't know the old arse could get his peterman up."

The girl came up, followed an instant later by Schulze. Immediately the Battle Group moved off, sticking to the shadows as best they could as tracer zipped lethally back and forth. Flares soared constantly into the burning sky to explode and hang there for a few moments before dropping like fallen angels. Up front van de Brug cursed. Perhaps the Ivans already knew about the escapes of this night and were on the lookout for them. He hoped he was wrong. The operation he intended to carry out was difficult enough. Goddamnit, it was!

They left the garden and started to cross the debris-littered Wilhelmstrasse, keeping a sharp lookout for shellholes which were everywhere. Up ahead van de Brug could just see the tail-end of the Kempka escape

119

group. So far they hadn't been spotted. He hoped his party's luck would hold out, too.

A star shell exploded directly above them. *"Freeze,"* he hissed urgently.

They stopped in their tracks, brains racing electrically, hearts thumping like triphammers. The flare hung there for what seemed an age, bathing their upturned faces in its icy, harsh, unfeeling light. Up ahead, Kempka's group had kept on going. Now the Russians somewhere in the smoking ruins spotted them. A slow enemy machine gun opened up, sounding like an irate woodpecker stabbing at a hard tree with its beak. Tracer sprayed the party. A woman screamed shrilly, hysterically, in sheer agony. Vaguely they heard Kempka yell, "Break up!" Then the lead party was scattering wildly in all directions, while the wounded woman screamed, "Oh please don't leave me . . . *For God's sake, don't leave me!"*

The star shell flare went out, leaving them blinking in the sudden darkness. A soldier prepared to move on, but van de Brug hissed urgently, "Don't move! Not yet. Till I give the word."

Next moment they saw the reason for his caution. Dark figures emerged from the ruins, darting from shadow to shadow, trying to reach the spot where the woman lay screaming.

"What are they going to do?" Heidi asked in a whisper.

Schulze knew what the Russians were going to do, but he didn't tell Heidi that. Instead he whispered back, "Loot the dead, I suppose. Most of those who went with the first group had valuables on them."

"Cut the cackle," van de Brug ordered sharply," We're moving again. *Los!"*

Behind them the wounded woman started to shriek,

"You can't do that to me . . . I'm wounded . . . *Bitte
. . . bitte . . . nein . . .*" Her voice died away suddenly
and was replaced by an animal grunting.

Heidi started to cry softly. They went on.

# SEVEN

Carefully, their shadows cast against the tiled walls of the underground tunnel by the lights of the torches they carried, the escapers picked their way through the debris which littered the lines. Others, many others, had gone before them. There was abandoned equipment, weapons, rucksacks, helmets, everywhere. Why the stuff had been abandoned, they did not know for certain, but they could guess. Somehow the Russians had got into the tunnel and frightened previous escapers into throwing away their gear so that they could run faster. So far, however, there had been no sign of the feared enemy.

Bringing up the rear, however, Schulze constantly fought the temptation to turn and look behind, carried away by an unreasoning fear that silent-footed Ivans were stalking them, just waiting for the opportunity to pounce. "Christ on a crutch," he told himself contemptuously more than once, "you're as nervous as a frigging old woman."

Up front, one of Wotan's veterans who had served with the Regiment in North Africa was singing a little drunkenly (something which Schulze envied for he hadn't had a drink since the Bunker and that was over half an hour ago) about "Dirty Gertie from Bizerte" who had a "mousetrap 'neath her skirtie" which "made her boyfriends most alerty". Schulze sighed enviously. He wished he had nerves like that.

Next to him, holding Heidi's hand, Matz said, "Where in three devils' name did that hairy-assed stubble-hopper get the firewater from, sod him?" He licked parched lips. "I could just do with a slug—" He stopped short and sniffed suspiciously. "What's that?" he exclaimed.

"What's what, plush ears?" Schulze barked and then he smelled it, too. The strong, cloying, sickly stench of petrol!

Up front van de Brug smelled it, too. He held up his good hand urgently. The long, well-strung-out column came to a ragged halt. "I'm going forward to investigate," he said to the man behind him. "Pass it on – quick."

Unslinging his machine gun, he crept forward, careful not to make the slightest noise, for he knew instinctively that something was wrong. Above them were the Russians, who probably knew by now that the underground leading to the Friedrichstrasse station was being used by escapers from the Führerbunker.

He advanced ten metres and then a further ten. Suddenly he saw it in the light of the torches being held by the men of the column. A shell probably had cracked the tiles overhead – he could see where the dead electric wires were hanging down in profusion, obviously severed by some sort of projectile. Now petrol was pouring through the cracks in a great stinking rain.

Van de Brug rubbed his unshaven chin. Where was it coming from? Perhaps from some shattered vehicle? But then he told himself even a tank wouldn't have that much fuel. The petrol was flooding down by the litre, as if it was being forced into the cracks from a pipe or tube. "Damn," he cursed out loud. Were the Ivans going to ignite the petrol soon and force whoever was down below out into the open? He guessed they were and, with the wind howling down the tunnel from the overhead Friedrichstrasse station some five hundred metres ahead around the bend, it would be like a gigantic blowtorch. They wouldn't stand a chance. No, he daren't take the risk.

Hurriedly he retraced his steps to where a worried Bormann and Kuehn were waiting. Swiftly he told them what he had seen and said, "I think it's a trap. We've got to get onto the surface as quickly as possible and make our way to the Friedrichstrasse station above ground. I can't run the risk of being caught in the tunnel when the Ivans fire that petrol."

"Agreed," Kuehn snapped urgently, wrinkling his nostrils at the stink of petrol. "But how?"

Bormann answered the question. "Every hundred metres, there's an inspection door, with stairs leading to the surface. The Führer ordered them installed after the Reichstag Fire of 1934."

Van de Brug didn't stop to ask why. Time was of the essence. The tunnel, reeking of petrol fumes now, was a firebomb just waiting to go off. "Come on," he cried. "Turn round and back up the tunnel. At the double!"

The urgency of his command infected them. The Wotan trooper paused in the middle of his drunken "She was voted in Bizerte, Miss Latrine for nineteen thirty." Then he, too, was stumbling and running with the rest back up the tunnel.

"There it is," Bormann, who had pushed himself into the lead, cried in near-panic. He stopped, chest heaving with the effort of running, and pointed a shaking finger at a small steel door set in the wall to the left.

"Good," van de Brug snapped. He strode over to the door swiftly and, grasping the handle, turned it. Nothing happened. The door didn't open.

"Here, let me try," Kuehn said urgently, as the fumes

came wafting towards them making the men cough and choke. Face red with suppressed rage, Kuehn seized the handle and turned it with all his strength. But again it refused to budge. The door simply would not open! "Shit," he cursed in English, "the goddamn son-of-a-bitch is locked from the other side." He wiped the sweat from his brow a little helplessly and added in German, "What now?"

Van de Brug shook his head. "I don't quite know. I don't want to go back to the entrance. That would be fatal. The Ivans will probably have captured it by now. We'd be walking right into their arms."

"Blow it, sir?" Schulze said calmly, knowing that a panic could break out at any moment, for all of them knew what their fate would be if the Russians ignited that flood of petrol which was already washing about their boots.

"Blow it," van de Brug echoed. "With what?"

"A bundle charge, sir. We strap three hand grenades together, tie them to the lock and then ignite them. That should do the trick."

"But then we risk that *we'll* ignite the petrol," van de Brug objected.

Schulze shrugged with apparent carelessness. "What's the alternative, sir?"

"You're right, Schulze." The Dutchman made his decision immediately. "You and you," he snapped to the two Wotan troopers nearest him. "Tie your grenades together with your belt. Hang them on the handle and then we'll fire a shot into them. That should do the trick . . . *Hurry!*"

Gently Matz pushed Heidi against the tiled wall with her face to it. "It's all right," he calmed her, seeing the look of fear in her eyes. "That big shit pal o' mine doesn't look if he's got penniworth o' brains, but he know what he's doing all right. Just keep your mouth open to stop your eardrums being burst by the blast." Numbly she did as he told her to do.

"All right, take cover everybody," van de Brug ordered. He turned to Schulze. "All right, it was your idea. Get on with it."

"Sir." Schulze licked his suddenly dry lips and raised his machine pistol. The petrol was already lapping over the tops of his boots. The stink was awful. He knew he was taking an awful risk of setting the whole tunnel ablaze. But the other alternative was just as dangerous. He took first pressure, knuckle white around the trigger. He pulled the trigger. The Schmeisser chattered at his side. Slugs howled off the steel. Suddenly, startlingly, the grenades went up. The hot blast hit him across the face. He blinked rapidly, vision blurred. Then everything came into focus once more.

The grenade had blown a ragged hole where the lock had been and now the door was swinging open on battered hinges.

Van de Brug didn't hesitate. "Come on," he yelled as the noise of the explosion echoed and re-echoed down the length of the petrol-filled tunnel. "This is our only chance!"

The deafened troopers needed no urging. They crowded into the fume-filled stairwell, peering upwards through the smoke. A winding steel staircase led upwards and disappeared into the gloom. Matz pushed Heidi to the front, crying above the racket, "Make way for an admiral there! Make way!"

Hastily Heidi started to clamber up the steps, followed by the others, fighting and jostling to get out before it was too late. Sergeant Schulze was just bringing up the rear when he heard it. A tremendous whoosh. A flash of blinding scarlet flame. Schulze reeled back as that tremendous heat hit him in the face. He fled to the stairs, kicking the door closed behind him with the heel of his boot. As he clattered up the steps, he could hear the paint on the far side crack and pop in the flames. Inside, too, the paint began to bubble and burst like the symptoms of some hideous skin disease. Slowly the steel started to glow a dull red.

Sweating all over, his clothes already beginning to smoulder, Schulze reached the second flight of the stairs leading upwards. Already Matz and a couple of the others were unscrewing the cover, frantic to get out before it was too late, with the others cursing or pleading, "Let us out . . . *for God's sake let us out!*"

Then the last screw was undone and the iron lid clattered onto the cobbles of the street. Fresh air streamed in as the greedy flames mounted and mounted up the stairwell, as if determined not to be deprived of their prey.

Matz put his hands on Heidi's pert little buttocks and pushed her out. Next moment he followed, too, and froze for a moment before grabbing her hand and crawling for cover. The others did the same as they saw what was going on in the street about a hundred metres away.

Just as a sweating, scorched, panting Schulze cleared the hole, van de Brug already had assessed the new situation. "Two T-34s still mobile, a handful of Ivan infantry and one knocked-out T-34. So far they haven't seen us. But it won't take long."

"*Shit, shit, shit,*" Matz cursed angrily. "Just got out of the frigging potato field and now we're back in the frigging taties. I . . ."

The rest of his angry outburst was drowned by the thud of a tank cannon. One of the stationary T-34s reared up on its bogies like a wild horse being put to harness for the first time. Immediately it started to burn fiercely, as the crew baled out, their uniforms already afire.

"That's one of ours," someone cried, new hope in his voice. "Look, the Russkis are backing off."

They were. The driver of the remaining tank had put his vehicle into reverse and covered by the infantry, the T-34 started to back off down the battle-littered street, the long, overhanging gun switching from side to side like some primeval monster ready to ward off an attack.

"Duck!" van de Brug ordered hurriedly.

As one they froze in the shadows as the tank and its accompanying infantry went by them. Hardly daring to breathe they waited until the Russians had disappeared around the bend, then van de Brug gave a swift signal. Without a word, they rose to their feet and moved on again. Bent and worn like weary old ghosts, they vanished into the gloom and fog of a dying Berlin, getting ever closer to their date with destiny.

# EIGHT

The Friedrichstrasse railway station was packed. Under the long shattered glass roof, hundreds, perhaps thousands of civilians waited for trains, which would now never come to take them to the West and safety. There were troops, young conscripts with pale undernourished faces, waiting for orders to attack outside, where and to what purpose nobody seemed to know. There were whores aplenty, being paid in cigarettes and slices of bread for taking the young men into the shadows where with their hands they satisfied them quickly and economically, giving them their last and perhaps only sexual thrill before they went to their deaths. There were officials running up and down with their clipboard still trying to appear important. There were "golden pheasants", Party officials known thus for their splendid uniforms with plenty of gold braid, begging, bribing, threatening, trying to escape before it was too late. And there were the wounded, long lines of them on their blood-soaked stretchers, moaning, quivering with fear as yet another Russian shell exploded nearby, crying for help to doctors who had long fled themselves.

Van de Brug had brought the survivors here, not because he needed the station but because he felt that there he'd get the latest information on the battle situation between there and the *Fabrik*. Five minutes before, he had sent off Bormann in his guise as a major-general in the SS to see the station commandant who would have that information, while he and Kuehn had withdrawn to the private office of railway transport officer to discuss what to do next. The Wotan troopers, for their part, had been ordered to remain on platform number five next to the once imposing entrance to the station to await further orders.

"Frig that for a lark," Schulze had snorted once the two officers had departed. "You feed the Miss," he beamed momentarily at Heidi, "while yours truly trots off to see if he can find some sauce, at least some suds." Now while an almost avuncular Matz – "you can call me Unkie, Miss, 'cos I know everything about yer – I've seen yer stark bollock naked" – fed the girl with his liver sausage sandwiches, Schulze "trotted off" to see what he could possibly scrounge.

\*   \*   \*

In the RTO's office, with the door locked and Kuehn facing it, his machine pistol at the ready resting across his lap, van de Brug said, a little worried, "It's not all going according to plan, but at least Bormann has the utmost confidence in us."

"Yes, the fool," Kuehn sneered, twin streams of cigarette smoke coming from his nostrils. "He'll learn soon enough what an arsehole he's been."

"Not so much of that, not just now at least," the Dutchman warned his fellow conspirator hastily. "Now, have you found out what he's carrying in the way of loot? We need to secure that before – well you know what."

"He's got something tucked away in his inside pocket. There are two packages, one square and even. I guess those are the greenbacks from which he gave you the five hundred bucks. By the way, check later if they're forged. I wouldn't put it past that slimeball."

Van de Brug nodded his agreement.

"The other is some kind of bag. I could feel it through the material." He frowned. "What do you think it could be?"

"Hm . . ." Van de Brug's brow wrinkled in a puzzled frown, as silence descended upon the locked office.

From outside there came the sound of a hysterical woman screaming, "I've lost my baby. He's only a toddler, just two, answers to the name of Dieter. Please help me . . . *Find Dieter!*"

"Silly cunt of a dame!" Kuehn snarled and lit another cigarette from the stub between his nicotine-stained fingers.

"What kind of a bag?"

"Don't know exactly. But what's in it," Kuehn answered, "is rough and a bit sharp-like."

Van de Brug snapped his fingers excitedly. "I've got it," he exclaimed. "Bormann has obviously planned this a long time. Think of the passports he provided us with – just like that. So, I conclude he's long had a foreign passport himself. Now, how would he finance himself when he did a bunk? He couldn't be carrying huge bundles of foreign currency and gold, the only things which count in Germany, in Europe today. So what else could he use?"

Kuehn's hard face lit up. "*Diamonds*, of course. The international currency. They'll take you anywhere these days."

"Yes," van de Brug agreed, his one eye flashing greedily, "and knowing Bormann, that bag won't just contain a few marks' worth. It'll be a fortune. Al," he chuckled, "we've hit the jackpot."

Forty or so metres away Schulze was having trouble

hitting any kind of pot. In the station restaurant, first class, naturally, the raddled blonde in her rusty black dress and dirty white apron, said indignantly, "What do you think this is, Sergeant, a better class knocking-shop or something? First we don't serve anybody under the rank of captain, and secondly we ain't got nothing to serve."

Schulze was undeterred. He knew the kind. He had been twisting them round his finger ever since he had first joined the Army – unwillingly. "By God," he breathed, "you're a devilishly handsome woman. Look at that kisser and what you've got in your blouse! What a pair. *Sugar.*" He kissed the tips of his fingers as he had seen Johannes Heesters do in the movies.

She looked at him hard. "You're not pulling my pisser?" she asked. "I'll be a grandma in three months' time – God willing."

"Grandma – *you?*" he exclaimed in mock surprise. "Impossible. You can't be a day over thirty."

She simpered. "Well I am, really am, though I admit I did get married very young, virtually a schoolgirl in short skirts." She fluttered her eyelashes at him.

Schulze knew he was winning. He had been this way before. "By God," he boomed, "and I bet you've wonderful legs under that – er – short skirt of yours. That's something to make a real man's heart beat faster." He assumed a serious mien. "But is there not somewhere more private where we can talk?" He touched her hand cautiously, looking very grave. "In times like these, one can't afford to waste much time. Life is too short."

Her eyelashes fluttered ever more rapidly. "How true . . . how true," she agreed. "Yes, there is. I have a little office at the back. Perhaps," she looked cautiously to left and right, "you would like a little something?"

His heart leapt. Already he could feel the "chinwater",

as he called it, begin to trickle down the sides of his mouth at the thought of the booze to come. He controlled himself. "But only if you will share a convivial drink with me, my little heart."

She actually flushed under the mask of powder and rouge. "Just a little," she conceded.

They went inside and she carefully locked the door behind her, saying, "We don't want any of that rabble outside bursting in when we're having out little drinkie, do we?" She smiled at him sweetly and sat down – carelessly.

"Holy cow," Schulze told himself as he looked at the massive, black-silk-clad thigh she now revealed, "I'm going to have to frigging pay for the suds!"

"Be so kind as to help yourself." She indicated the stone bottle of best Westphalian schnapps on the table. "The glasses are in the cupboard, and please be so kind as to pour me a little one."

"I am at your command," Schulze responded gallantly with a little bow, eyes lighting up at the sight of the bottle. He turned and, opening the cupboard, reached in for the glasses, noting as he did so that there was another bottle of schnapps next to them. When he turned round again, he saw, too, that her tight skirt had ridden up even higher to reveal an expanse of naked white flesh above the red lace garters which held up her stockings. He said nothing. Instead he poured two generous portions of schnapps and raised his glass in toast. "Bottoms up," he chortled.

She giggled. "Oh, you naughty man, that's all you soldiers ever think about, isn't it!" She downed the whole glassful in one go. "I think I'll have another one," she breathed, holding out the empty glass, "before you have your wicked way with me."

Schulze sighed and drained his own glass, telling himself

that a man had to go through quite a lot to get a little drink. He reached for the stone bottle . . .

"The station commandant says," Bormann said a little breathlessly, for he had just managed to escape being given the command of a group of leaderless SS men that a junior and very eager officer had wanted to take into action against the "Jewish Bolsheviks", "that *Fabrik* is still holding out. He was in contact with the battalion commander there by radio some ten minutes ago."

"Excellent," van de Brug said. "And what did he say of the situation to the direct front of the station, between it and the *Fabrik* post?"

"Strangely quiet," Bormann replied. "He had been expecting an attack from an area of parkland to the left of the station, but it didn't come. All he's been getting since darkness fell is the odd infantry and tank attack, of the kind we saw on our way here. And he still has four or five Tiger tanks left which can deal with that kind of an attack easily."

Van de Brug and Kuehn considered for a few moments, trying not to hear the noises coming from outside, the crying babies, the high-pitched hysterical voices of the frustrated women, the harsh commands of the military police trying to keep order, the moans and pleas of the abandoned wounded. The end was near at the Friedrichstrasse station and they had get out of the place soon.

"I'd go for the parkland, Piet." Kuehn broke the silence first. "It'll give us room for manoeuvre in case—" He left the rest of the sentence unfinished.

Van de Brug nodded. "Yes, I think that's the best route to the *Fabrik* post. In the streets we could well be easily trapped. All right give the men another five minutes' rest and then we leave."

Kuehn went out and van de Brug turned to Bormann. "*Reichsleiter*, from now onwards until we reach the safety of the West, I want you to obey my orders implicitly." He looked at the Party boss hard with his one keen eye. "I want no questions. 'Why?' and 'where?' etc. are out. Just do as you are told. Undoubtedly you will see things that will surprise you greatly." He gave the other man a hard, knowing smile.

Bormann told himself that the Dutchman might think he was in command and he'd allow him to think thus. But when the time came and he was in safety it would be his turn to give the orders. The two SS thugs might think he was just a fat stupid civilian, but in his time he had murdered men in cold blood. He could do it again. He still had a trick or two up his sleeve. Aloud, he said, "Anything you say, *Hauptsturm*. I am totally at your command . . ."

# NINE

"Phew!" Schulze sighed and, wiping the sweat off his brow, offered the bottle to Matz. "You don't frigging well know what I had to do to get that firewater, so go easy on it."

Matz licked his lips greedily, wiped the neck of the bottle daintily and raised it to his lips, while Schulze watched him carefully.

Outside the station to the left where the park area was, all seemed silent save for the odd flare ascending into the sky, in contrast with the rest of the city which was racked with violent action. At any other time Sergeant Schulze would have been suspicious: the park was *too* quiet. But at that particular moment his mind was still full of the big woman's demands. By the second drink she had been on top of him, knickers off, straddling his lower body with those great heavy thighs of her, crying in a strangled voice, "*Stick it to me . . . come on stick it to me! I can't wait to get all of it inside me, you great beast, you!*"

Three minutes later, lathered in sweat and panting as if he had just run a great race, he thought he had taken care of her for that night. He had been mistaken. He had hardly wiped himself, when she was at him again, pulling at his flaccid organ with a look of manic desire in her eyes, mouth open and drooling. "It's not a frigging garden hose, you know," he had protested, but she had not been listening. She had continued; she had produced the effect she desired. Then she had thrown herself on top of him once more, writhing and groaning, banging herself up and down upon him, as if she were galloping a frisky stallion. He had only been allowed to go when van de Brug had shrilled his whistle and cried, "Battle Group van de Brug stand to!" His last sight of her had been the woman standing at the door, naked from the waist downwards, rubbing the base of her stomach as if she had an insatiable itch, and crying, "How naughty of you to leave a girl just when she's starting to get aroused." He'd fled.

Now recovered a little, he pulled the precious bottle away from Matz, stowed it in his pocket and turning to Heidi, said, "Now remember, stick with me and Corporal Matz. And remember, as I told you before, it's not only the Ivans we've got to watch out for, it's those three shits up front." He pointed a finger like a small, hairy sausage at Bormann and the foreign SS officers. "They're up to no good, take it from me."

"Thank you, Sergeant Schulze and you, too, Corporal Matz," the girl said sweetly. "What have I done to deserve such good friends?"

Corporal Matz, that veteran of hundreds of whore-houses in a dozen different countries, actually blushed.

Now they advanced through the glowing darkness of the park, rifles and weapons held across their chests at the high port, each man tense and expectant, bent forward slightly, as if walking against a stiff breeze. Flares continued to explode in the air to the front. But there was no sign of the enemy in the park itself. It had been left to them and the stray pets, cats and dogs, which, frightened by the shelling and bombing, now wandered around aimlessly, trying to find their old masters. But in most cases they were dead, buried in the ruins of the wrecked houses that surrounded the park.

For a while some kind of a mongrel tried to keep up with them, whining pitifully as it tried to curry favour until finally, with a curse, Kuehn launched a kick at it. The creature ran off howling into the darkness. But not for long. A second later there was a tremendous bang which stopped them in their tracks. The dog howled piteously one last time, then with a moan it died.

"What in three devils' name was that?" Bormann exclaimed, shocked and not a little frightened.

The two officers didn't answer his question. They couldn't. They did not know what had caused the dog's death.

But Schulze did. "Mines," he called. "It ran over a mine."

Next to him Heidi stiffened fearfully and Schulze pressed her arm reassuringly.

"So that's why there was no sign of the Ivans in the park," van de Brug said bitterly.

"What are we going to do?" Bormann asked. "I mean we can't get through a minefield, can we?" He looked enquiringly at van de Brug.

The Dutchman didn't conceal his contempt for the frightened Party officer. "*You* can't," he snapped, his mind racing to meet the new challenge. "*We* can. Because *we've* got guts!"

"Sergeant Schulze," van de Brug turned and called.
"Sir?"

"Take two men and see what you can do about clearing a path about one metre broad."

"Yessir," Schulze answered promptly. He had done this sort of thing before, but he didn't like it all the same. "Matzi, you stay with the girl."

138

"But you'll need me."

"No buts and cover me back as well while you're at it," Schulze snapped. "All right. You, Hartmann and you, Terboven." Both men were "old hares". They knew what to do immediately.

Schulze drew his bayonet and went on his knees. Hartmann did the same to his right and Terboven to his left. "Right, off we go," Schulze said and prodded the earth to his immediate front. "And keep your eyes peeled."

"Like skinned tomatoes, Sarge," Hartmann said cheekily and did the same.

Now, while the others crouched and waited at the edge of the Russian-laid minefield, the three men advanced at a snail's pace, prodding the earth systematically to a width of one metre, clearing a path big enough for a man to walk through safely.

"What exactly are they doing?" Heidi asked fearfully, gripping Corporal Matz's arm till it hurt.

"Well, if the point of their bayonet strikes something metallic under the earth, they know they've found a mine. They come in two kinds," Matz went on, "anti-tank and anti-personnel. It's those little buggers, if you'll pardon my French, which cause the trouble. Some just blow off your foot. But there are older frigging ones which loose off a load of steel balls to the height of a bloke's crotch. Anyone who gets hit by one of them ain't no good in bed with his missus any more."

Heidi shivered and said. "I hope Sergeant Schulze will be careful."

"Oh, they say, weeds never decay. Old Schulzi'll be all right," Matz said with more conviction than he felt.

The minutes ticked by in tense apprehension, with everyone unconsciously waiting for that first explosion which would spell disaster for one of the three men out on their knees.

Sweating like pigs, each new move made only by a conscious effort of sheer willpower, hardly daring to breathe, the three men dug and dug, waiting for that first startling, frightening scrape of metal against metal.

Schulze was first to stumble onto something. There it was – the point of his bayonet rasping against steel. "Stop," he commanded in a voice he barely recognized as his own, "got one!"

They stopped dead.

Gingerly Schulze lowered his bayonet and in the glowing darkness, started to brush the earth from the mine. "Phew," he sighed after a few moments, "it's anti-tank. All right, boys, let's move on." But even as he spoke, he wondered when they would come across the first anti-personnel mines, always used by the Russian sappers to cover the bigger mines to prevent the enemy from lifting them.

The minutes ticked by. They had cleared a path of some fifty metres deep now and van de Brug alerted the men to be ready to start following them soon. Next to Heidi, Matz, very tense and nervous, not taking his eyes off the crawling men for a moment, said in a dry, cracked voice, "But the Ivans are up to all sorts of little tricks, nasty little tricks, with mines. These days they are making them of wood, even glass, so that you can't find them with a mine detector. Even when you do, they can still play tricks on yer, if you don't watch it. Sometimes they put another charge shaped like a matchbox – you know those books of matches they use to give away with Juno cigarettes before the war?"

Heidi nodded her understanding.

"Well, if you ain't in the know, you lift the mine and

140

the charge underneath goes off – then you have no face and hands and are blinded. Or they attach a wire from one mine to another. Lift either one and the other goes up just metres away – and you're probably dead."

Heidi shivered violently. "How terrible! I never knew war was like that."

"War's hell," Matz said laconically. "Sheer hell."

"*Anti-personnel!*" Schulze, in the lead, sang out suddenly.

There was a shocked gasp. The two men behind him stopped where they were, frozen as if for eternity. This was it.

Carefully, very carefully, Schulze cleared the earth around the top of the mine, which looked like a tin of "old man", the standard German meat ration reputedly made from the bodies of old men culled from Berlin's workhouses. Three wire hooks were revealed. Schulze gave a soft sigh. Put a finger on any one of those, he knew, and it would be curtains.

He buried his fingers into the soft earth. He crooked them underneath the mine, telling himself that half an hour before he had been crooking his fingers into holes far more pleasant than this. But that was already history. Now the sweat was standing out on his forehead in great opaque pearls. Nothing. There was no booby-trap beneath the anti-personnel mine.

He probed further, searching for a thin wire leading from this mine to another one. Again nothing. He sucked in a deep breath. Gingerly, very gingerly, hardly able to control the trembling of his right hand, he reached for the fuse cap. Forcing himself to take his time, he started to unscrew it.

He didn't get far. Hartmann, trying to relax from his strained position, put out one hand to steady himself. It was the last move he ever made. The hand hit the prong. He knew instantly what he had done. *"God in heaven!"* he began. But it was too late. The mine exploded. His whole left side was ripped apart, the metal tearing off his flesh as if it was paper to reveal the gleaming white ribs beneath. He fell slowly, very slowly, to one side. The next moment the Russian machine gun covering the minefield, just waiting for this to happen, opened up, and van de Brug was screaming above the racket, *"Run for* it *. . . fuck the mines, RUN FOR IT!"*

# TEN

There were just ten of them left now, apart from Schulze, Matz, Heidi, the two foreign officers and Bormann. Both Hartmann and Terboven, plus six others, were dead and dying, left behind as they had fled through the minefield, mines exploding in bright flashes of flame and soil to left and right, the Russian machine gun scything the park with its fire.

Weary, miserable, feeling a little hopeless, they slumped in the cover of the hedge at the far end of the park, sobbing for breath, hardly knowing what to do next. It seemed that for the last few days of this terrible April that they had been running in and out of the frying pan all the time; that there was no hope for them, however hard they tried.

Schulze sensed his men's mood. He licked his parched lips and said, "I know lads, it seems as if we've always got our hooters in the shit. But even shit-shovellers do manage to get away from the crap now and again. We're gonna too, I promise you that by the Great Whore of Buxtehude where the dogs piss through their ribs!"

A couple of weary men said, "Good old Schulze. He'll see us through."

Matz, however, was unimpressed. "Pull the other one, Schulzi," he snorted. "It's got frigging bells on it. Ner, what we've got to do is to pack this frigging thing in, here and now. There's no sense in it. Let's just sling our hook, get out of the dust while there's still time, 'cos if we don't do something soon, we'll be looking up at the taties from two metres below the ground."

"Button yer frigging lips," Schulze hissed urgently. "You don't want that lot to hear." He indicated the officers and Bormann who crouched a little way off from the Wotan troopers. "Or do you fancy a bullet in yer back?"

Heidi said, "Do you think they'd do that, Sergeant Schulze?" Again she was frightened.

"Yes," he answered simply. "But don't worry, nothing's going to happen to you – or us." There was new determination in his voice suddenly. "Arses-with-ears like that lot'll have to get up much earlier in the morning if they want to catch Mrs Schulze's handsome son out." He beckoned the rest of the troopers to come closer and when they were, he whispered, "Look, lads, this is what I know. When – and if – we reach the *Fabrik*, those three," he indicated the two officers and Bormann, "are going to take over a truck there and do a bunk, leaving us to piss in the wind. Well, they've got another think coming. *We're* taking that truck and we're heading west out of this mess. But till then we've got to watch our backs. Forget the Ivans and keep yer glassy orbs fixed on them three. Clear?"

"Clear, Schulze," came a murmur of assent from the others, who now stared at the dark shapes of the officers as if they were seeing them for the very first time.

Five minutes later the order came to move out once more. Van de Brug said, "With a bit of luck we should reach *Fabrik* just before dawn. From there things should be a lot easier. The infantry battalion can give us covering fire and then we'll be off again, heading for the Havel."

The men listened obediently enough, but said nothing as they slipped out of their cover and began to move down

144

the street in the shadow of the ruined houses, fingers ready on the triggers of their weapons. For all of them knew the Russians were close again. Tension lay heavy in the air. Even Matz was affected. He shivered, as an icy finger of fear traced its way slowly down his spine and he said almost apologetically, "A louse must have run across my liver."

"More likely you're about to cream yer drawers," Schulze said, but without rancour. For he, too, felt an eerie sense of foreboding, as if trouble, exactly what he didn't know, was lying in wait for them at the very next corner.

The minutes slipped by. The sounds of battle had grown muted, as if both sides had now settled down for the night, weary of the slaughter. Somewhere a dog began to howl at the red moon. A slight breeze sprang up. The paper which lay everywhere, letters, bits of newspapers, looted documents, started to drift noisily up and down the ruined street. A horse without a rider cantered by, not seeing the men slipping through the shadows. Matz wasn't an imaginative man, but all the same, he felt as if he was in some kind of waking dream. The howling dog, the drifting paper, the cantering horse – they all seemed so unreal. Again he shivered violently and Heidi at his side whispered, concerned, "Are you all right, dear Corporal Matz?"

"Of course I am, *Fraulein*," he assured her, but without conviction.

Five minutes later they bumped into the Gestapo execution squad and knew that they had reached the safety of what German defences were left. There were half a dozen of them, middle-aged, cynical-looking men in ankle-length leather coats which creaked every time they shot one of the prisoners. There was a fat granny who had "organized" a sack of coal from a bombed-out

145

cellar. A pale-faced, skinny soldier who had apparently deserted from "a stomach battalion", composed entirely of soldiers who had stomach problems . . .

The Gestapo men, all of them with stumps of cigars clamped between their gold teeth, rattled off the usual formula, "In the name of the Führer and the German Folk, this specially convened court sentences you to death." A burst of machine-gun fire and the victim fell dead in the gutter.

An ugly girl, sitting in the rubble with her fat legs apart so that they could see the soft white flesh of her thighs above the shabby darned stockings, was about to be shot when they came on the scene. "What have you to say for yourself, bitch?" the biggest of the Gestapo men rasped, rolling his cheap cigar from one side of his thick-lipped mouth to the other.

"Fuck off," the ugly girl said without any real animosity. "Right you are, bitch," the Gestapo man cried. He pressed the trigger of his Schmeisser. Flame spat from its muzzle. A sudden line of red buttonholes ran the length of her bulging breasts. The ugly girl flew backwards and sprawled dead on the bricks.

Heidi shrieked and hid her head.

The Gestapo man suddenly became aware of them. He spotted Bormann in the uniform of a major-general of the SS and clicked to attention. "Beg to report, sir," he barked, as if he were back on some peacetime parade ground. "Special Secret Police Detachment Five dealing with deserters and defeatists." He swung Bormann a tremendous salute.

Bormann returned it, saying, "You are doing excellent work. We must stamp out this sort of thing before the rot sets in. What's he done?" He pointed to someone who looked like a clergyman, whose face was swollen and red, with one eye turning black, seeming as if he had been recently knocked about.

"Cocky bastard, sir. Found him in a cellar writing on the wall, that the 'Lord must forgive the German people for their crimes'." He sneered contemptuously. "Now we're going to allow him to join his frigging Lord sooner than he expected, eh, sir?" He laughed.

Bormann laughed, too.

The clergyman started to pray, his eyes tightly closed like a child, trying to blot out some painful sight, as the Gestapo man raised his Schmeisser once more.

Schulze saw red suddenly. "Drop that frigging gun, you shit-arsed bull!" he roared.

The Gestapo man's mouth dropped open foolishly. "Did you speak to me, Sergeant?" he stuttered. As long as he had been in the dreaded Gestapo no one had ever dared talk to him like that.

"Who the frig do you think I'm talking to?" Schulze rasped menacingly, levelling his own weapon at the policeman's fat belly. "Drop that thing or you'll be eating lead."

"*Stop that, Schulze!*" Kuehn cried, as the parson opened his eyes and blinked, as if he were wondering why he was still alive.

Matz levelled his own Schmeisser. "Keep out of this," he snapped warningly. Around him the rest of the Wotan troopers raised their weapons. They knew where their first loyalty lay.

"Why . . . why," Kuehn was abruptly taken off guard, "this is mutiny!"

"No," Schulze shouted, "it's frigging reason, that's what it is. Hey, you, Bible-thumper, off you go while there's still time. Beat it!"

The parson looked from one group to the other, wondering if he could trust anyone. Then he was off, doubling away into the glowing darkness as fast as his feet could carry him.

Schulze waited till he had vanished, then he snarled, "All right, bulls, drop those popguns of yours. *Quick!*" He made a threatening gesture with his Schmeisser.

The middle-aged cops saw he was serious. They unbuckled their pistol belts and dropped them on the rubble next to the dead granny and the ugly woman. Reluctantly the big Gestapo man followed suit, tossing his Schmeisser away. "You'll pay for this," he said through gritted teeth.

"Hold yer water, bull," Schulze said. "You can't seem to realise – all of you—" his gaze embraced Bormann and the two SS officers "—that you're finished, done for. Now you're nobodies, without any power any more. Go on, fart-in-the-wind, get moving before I really lose my temper." He pressed the trigger of his Schmeisser. Bullets beat a tattoo in the rubble near the big killer's boots. He got the message. He broke into a clumsy run. The others followed, while the Wotan troopers watched, faces hard and vengeful.

For what seemed a long time, they remained rooted thus, the heavy, brooding silence broken only by the rattle of machine-gun fire a long way off, each man wrapped up in a cocoon of his own thoughts and fears. Then van de Brug flashed Kuehn a significant look before crying, "All right, let's move out, while we can."

The Wotan troopers shook themselves like men finding it hard to awaken from a heavy sleep. Shoulders slumped, as if in defeat, they started to follow the two officers and Bormann through the rubble. Matz, Heidi and Schulze brought up the rear. Matz shot Schulze a look just before they left. It said, *Watch your back from now on, Schulzi – you're a marked man.*

Half an hour later, they reached *Fabrik*. It was still in German hands and as they trooped into the courtyard Matz and Schulze could see that the little truck was still in place under its camouflage netting with a guard in front of it.

The actors were in place, the scene was set, the last stage of the drama could commence . . .

# PART THREE

# *March or Croak*

"Buy combs, lads, there are lousy times ahead."

*The Sayings of Sergeant Schulze*

# ONE

It was two hours after they had escaped from the Russians, that van de Brug and Kuehn made their decision. The Russian infantry had launched a surpise attack on the SS positions to the east of Berlin in the middle of the night. "*Urrah . . . urrah!*" they cried excitedly, as they came out of the night, firing from the hip as they did so. The sentries and lookouts were overwhelmed at once. Here and there in the foxholes, some of the weary SS troopers managed to wake up to meet the attack. But mostly they were bayonetted to death or had their throats cruelly slit before they had had time to open their eyes.

Kuehn and van de Brug had been with half a dozen other SS officers of the French SS division "*Charlemagne*" sleeping in the hay of a ruined barn, when the Russians had commenced tossing in grenades. A phosphorus grenade had exploded in a burst of intense white flame on the floor. The hay had caught fire immediately. The heat had been just too much. "*Ruki verk!*" the Russians had cried harshly. "*Davoi . . . davoi.*"

Van de Brug had looked at the terrified French officers and had said, a note of resignation in his voice, as the flames leapt higher and higher, "We have no other choice. It's got to be surrender."

*Obersturmbannführer* Marchand had cried, "But they'll shoot us out of hand! They always do with SS officers."

"*Davoi!*" the harsh command in Russian had cut into his plea.

So they had filed out, hands in the air as commanded. The Russians had started to beat and cuff them immediately, looting them of everything, watches, rings, money, wallets, before pushing and shoving them roughly to a large truck which had turned out to be a mobile HQ. Faces swollen and already beginning to turn green and black from the beatings, blood trickling down from their smashed noses, their interrogation had commenced at once.

The interrogator was a small, dark commissar with keen sharp eyes glistening from behind the gold pince-nez he affected. "A kike," Kuehn told himself. He had always been able to recognize kikes ever since he had been a kid in short pants in his native Brooklyn.

The little Jew wasted no time. In excellent German, he snapped, "I have no time to loose. I have three questions to ask of you and I want them answered *immediately!*" Hurriedly he translated what he had just said in Russian for the benefit of the big, burly, shaven-skulled colonel sitting impassively next to him, smoking a long Russian cigarette

The little Jew snapped, "Now, these are the questions. Where is the divisional HQ of the SS *Charlemagne* Division? What is the division's approximate strength? What is your current battle plan?" He rapped out the questions, jaw working as if on a taut steel spring. He pointed to Marchand. "You are the senior man. You answer."

Marchand's face was ashen, but shook his head and said in a tight, little voice, "I refuse to answer."

The commissar didn't hesitate. "Then you will be shot." He said something to the guards. Hurriedly a couple of them grabbed Marchand by the arms, pulling him outside down the steps that led into the truck. There was the rattle of a tommy gun's shrill scream and then silence. Marchand was dead.

The Jew didn't speak for a moment. He let the knowledge of what had just happened to the French SS officer sink in. Then he said, "You must remember that your lives are forfeit. Not only are you officers of the criminal SS, but you are also traitors and renegades, with no future, absolutely no future, in Europe. There is no place where you will be able to hide once Germany has lost the war, which will be soon. Now answer my questions. *You.*" He pointed to the French officer standing next to Al Kuehn.

The young lieutenant swallowed hard. He was obviously afraid of death, but he had his pride. He opened his mouth, but nothing came.

"Hurry up," the little Jew snapped. "Or you'll be dead in sixty seconds—"

His words ended in a sudden yelp of pain, as van de Brug hit him with his wooden hand. He reeled backwards, as Kuehn sprang over the table and grabbed the big shaven-headed colonel's pistol out of his holster and held it against the man's left temple. The guards stopped in their tracks. Kuehn grinned evilly. The tables had been turned neatly. He kicked the Jew, who was bleeding badly. "Kike, tell them to drop their weapons. *Quick!*" He eased the trigger of the pistol back threateningly.

The commissar said something thickly in Russian. Reluctantly the men unslun their tommy guns and put them on the floor of the truck. The French officers didn't need a second invitation. They grabbed the weapons, as van de Brug said quickly, "All right, kick 'em outside. We'll keep the big Ivan as an hostage, and the Jew. You," he snapped to the young French officer, "you can drive this thing. You go with him as an escort."

Minutes later, followed by a volley of angry fire, they were on their way, tearing through the night as if the Devil himself was behind them.

Just before dawn they had run out of fuel. Again van de Brug had made the right decision. "We'll shoot the two Ivans," he announced, his voice without emotion as if he passed sentences of death every day, "then we'll split up. Kuehn, you will come with me."

Kuehn had grinned knowingly. He knew and the Dutchman knew, too, that the French officers would stick together. It was something that the French always did. If the Ivans were looking for them, they'd find the larger number of Frenchmen first. It might deflect the chase from them.

Five minutes later and the Jew and the Russian colonel were sprawled out at the roadside, both dead with the backs of their heads blown off by Al Kuehn, and they were on their way, leaving the road for the forest which bordered it, marching up the heights as far as the eye could see.

That afternoon as they crouched in a thick growth of resin-scented pines, listening to the faint, sudden burst of firing which might indicate the Russians had found the French officers, van de Brug had come up with his idea. "That little Yid was right, of course, Al," he said thoughtfully as the firing ceased. "There is no place left in Europe for us to go."

Kuehn nodded his understanding. "Yes, I suppose you've hit the nail on the head, Piet. The States are out as well. They're too far away anyway."

"Nowhere is too far away providing you have money," van de Brug had countered after some thought.

All was silent now save for the lazy buzz of the flies in the mild spring sunshine which cut through the branches into their hiding place. The war could have been a million miles away. But both of them knew it was close enough, too damned close. "But where are we going to get a lot of money, Piet?" Kuehn said after a while. "We could rob a bank I suppose. But the banks would probably only have Reichsmarks and what good are they today? What we need is foreign currency. Greenbacks, Limey pounds, stuff like that."

"I agree and there is one place where there will still be foreign currency. Berlin." The Dutchman looked at his comrade and could see new hope spreading across his dirty, tough, unshaven face.

"Yes, of course," the latter said. "The government would have to keep some kind of foreign money in the capital to buy things for the war effort. But how could we break into the Reichsbank, for example, and get away with it?"

Van de Brug lowered his voice, as if he were afraid of being heard even here in this lonely forest. "But we wouldn't need to break into a bank, Al," he said carefully, as if his ideas were developing in his mind as he expressed them. "There's the Chancellery."

Kuehn whistled softly. "That's aiming high, isn't it?"

"We're SS officers. We have easy access and you can imagine what the state of the place will be now, with the Ivans closing in on all sides. The big shots will all be preparing to do a bunk before it's too late – Himmler, Fat Hermann" – he meant the enormous, fat Hermann Goering, the commander of the *Luftwaffe* – "Goebbels and the like. And all of them will be taking something other than useless marks with them. Perhaps a couple of old masters, dollars and pounds, perhaps jewels – things

157

like that. All we've got to do is to get our greedy paws on something like that and we can buy our freedom anywhere outside Europe."

The happy look which had begun to animate Kuehn's face vanished suddenly. "Yer, that's the catch, Piet," he said swiftly.

"What do you mean?

"That kind of stuff would certainly buy us a hide-out in – say – some South American banana republic. Money talks in places like that. But we'd have to get out of Europe first. Every escape route we could take is blocked by the goddamn enemy. The Yanks and Limeys are everywhere in Western Europe. Say, for instance, we tried to get to neutral Spain and find a ship or plane there, we'd have to cover hundreds of miles through France. Possibly we could grease a few Frog palms there, but not *all* of them. Then we'd be for the chop at double-smart time. They'd string us, two SS officers, up on the nearest lamppost."

Van de Brug had sighed. He stroked the bristles of his chin and said slowly, "You've got a point there." He was silent for a while, as Kuehn crouched there next to him, wishing for a slug of good honest bourbon. He certainly needed it this day, for his reason told him after the narrow brush with sudden death the previous night, time was running out for men like him. He had fought in North Africa, Sicily, Italy and then France with the "Big Red One"* and come through without a scratch. Now it looked pretty certain that he might well end up in Fort Leavenworth, being strung up by his own former comrades, if they didn't come up with an idea that would work pretty soon

* The US 1st Infantry Division, named thus after the red first numeral of its divisional patch.

158

It was then that van de Brug had come up with his amazing suggestion. For a long while after he had made it, the American stared at him aghast. "But," he stuttered finally, breaking the heavy afternoon silence, "we'll . . . never get away with it, Piet!"

Van de Brug had looked him hard with that one eye of his and had replied calmly, as if it were a fact of life. "We will. We *have* to. From now onwards, Al, it is going to be the old SS motto – *march or croak*." He rose to his feet. "Come on, Al, we've got to get to Berlin."

# TWO

"*Stormoviks!*" the air sentry cried in alarm. He lowered his binoculars and immediately began cranking the handle of the air-raid siren.

The *Fabrik* came to life with startled suddenness. The weary infantrymen threw themselves out of their sleeping places and grabbed their weapons. They had been expecting this final all-out attack for days now. On this May 1st, 1945, the Ivans were coming at last. It was going to be the final battle.

Their silver wings glistening in the dawn sun, the Russian dive-bombers seemed to hover virtually motionless in the hard blue sky, as they pinpointed their target. Behind their machine guns, the infantry tensed and waited, squinting into the sun.

The Russian squadron leader wiggled his wings. It was the signal.

"Here the shits come!" someone shouted in alarm. The gunners tensed. Suddenly, startlingly, the first Stormovik fell out of the sky. Sirens howling hideously, engine snarling it screamed downwards, as if intent on smashing itself to pieces on the ground below. Tracer fire crossed and criss-crossed, trying to bar its path. To no avail! It howled through the fire at five hundred kilometres an hour.

The Stormovik jerked abruptly. It was as if it had

160

just run into an invisible wall. It trembled. A myriad
deadly little eggs tuubled from its blue-painted belly
in crazy profusion. Schulze crossed himself with mock
solemnity. "Thank God for what we are about to receive,"
he intoned and then ducked as the first bombs came
shrieking down.

A stick ran the whole length of the front of the
factory. Masonry shivered, groaned and came falling
down in a slither of shattered brick and dust. The
Stormovik pilot flattened out and went barrelling away
at top speed.

The second dive-bomber followed. Again the shriek
of sirens, the ear-splitting howl of engines, followed an
instant later by a shower of bombs and incendiaries.

The ground heaved and trembled like a live thing.
"God save me, please," Heidi whimpered fearfully,
as she crouched in the shelter of the courtyard wall.
Matz, his arm around her skinny shoulders protectively,
reassured her. "Don't worry, *Fraulein*," he said hastily.
"Bark's worse than the bite. Believe me, you'll be all
right . . ." The rest of his words were drowned by the
sharp dry cracks of the incendiary bombs exploding. A
moment later came the searing, blinding white flash of
phosphorus bursting into flames. Suddenly the air was
depleted of oxygen as the fires raged, making them gasp
and pant like ancient asthmatics.

Now the Russians poured the full weight of their aerial
artillery on the garrison of the *Fabrik*, while further away
the guns started to thunder, an indication that they would
be soon launching a full-scale infantry assault on the
factory.

Schulze scuttled over to Matz and Heidi. He held his
mouth close to his old running mate's ear, as yet another
dive-bomber fell out of the burning sky. "Matzi, old

house, get ready to move out. Get the chaps ready. I think this is *it*."

"What about the cheesehead and the *Ami* . . ." The rest of Matz's question was drowned by a sudden roar as the truck under the camouflage net reared up in the air. A tyre exploded. Next moment the petrol tank went up. The precious truck had been hit. In an instant it was burning fiercely.

Schulze forced a grin. "Now the shitehawks have lost their wheels," he shouted almost gleefully. "See what his nibs," he meant van de Brug, "will frigging do now?" He ran back across the shrapnel-littered yard.

"*Shit on the shingle!*" van de Brug cursed angrily in German, as he raised himself from his cover and saw the truck burning fiercely. "That's put the clock in the pisspot!"

Bormann, his face ashen and frightened, looked from him to Kuehn in absolute confusion. "What . . . what are we going to do now, please?" he asked, a note of pleading in his voice.

For a moment van de Brug was at a loss. He didn't know. Already he could hear the cries of the Russian infantry, full of vodka, preparing for the assault, shouting, "*Slava Krasnaya Armya*" – long live the Red Army. It wouldn't be long now.

Kuehn found the answer for him. "We still need those hairy-assed Wotan troopers," he said swiftly, as suddenly the truck which would have taken them to the Havel disintegrated in one final explosion. "We'll have to take them that far. A bribe. Perhaps ten dollars each should do the trick." He turned and looked hard at a pensive van de Brug. "But we've got to watch that big arsehole – what's his name, Schulze. I think he's tumbled to us."

"I think he has," van de Brug agreed, rousing himself

from his lethargy, as the rest of the Stormoviks vanished, winging their way eastwards, and Russian artillery shells began to fall in the factory area. "But first things first. Let's get out of this death trap."

"Won't the infantry major object?" Bormann asked.

The Dutchman looked at him as if he were some village idiot. "Haven't you got all your cups in yer cupboard, Bormann?" he asked cynically. "The man's been bribed with your dollars. As soon as he can he's gonna take a dive himself. His battalion can make out the best it can without him. The whole crappy shoot is falling apart."

Bormann looked aghast. His previous confidence that he could manage the business of escaping without the two foreigners was shaken a little. Still, he told himself, using the old German proverb, "the left hand must scratch the right". If he couldn't use van de Brug and the Ami, what about this big fellow Schulze. He looked like a bit of a simpleton. He should be easy to manipulate; easy for buying for "an apple and an egg", as they said in his native Mecklenberg. "I see," he said shortly.

"You don't," van de Brug sneered contemptuously. "But you will. Never fear, we'll get you of this shitty mess. All right, prepare to move out once the artillery bombardment has ceased. That will mean the Russian infantry attack has started."

"*Jawohl*," Bormann answered in his new humility, though he kept his bull-like head bent so that the other two couldn't see the look in his dark eyes.

"All right," Schulze bellowed above the thunder of the Russian guns and rockets, "We're going to take a powder, lads, once the barrage ceases. Those whiteheels still need us now that their truck is burnt out, but watch yer backs. You can't trust them as far as yer throw 'em."

As abruptly as it had started the barrage ceased, leaving

behind it a loud echoing silence. "*Urrah . . . urrah!*" came the first faint cheers of the Russian infantry advancing, high on pepper vodka and looted schnapps. Schulze shook his head. The Ivans didn't seem to know what a creeping barrage was with the infantry advancing behind a rolling bombardment of shells. The result was that their infantry always attacked unprotected by their own guns. Well, that wasn't his headache, he told himself.

All around now the infantry were popping up in their foxholes and slit trenches, preparing to meet the attackers. Mostly they were very young or very old, the last scrapings of the barrel. "Poor bastards," Matz cursed. "A load of cardboard, Christmas-tree soldiers – cannon-fodder."

Schulze nodded his agreement. "Nothing we can do about it, Matzi. But they'll do one good thing – they'll cover our withdrawal." He unslung his machine pistol and tapped the long magazine to check if it were securely in place. It was. "All right, Matzi, start leading 'em out and watch the *Fraulein*."

"Will do," Matz answered dutifully and waved for the survivors to follow him. Schulze remained where he was, Schmeisser held across his chest. To his front the Russians, in their long flapping overcoats, were breaking into an awkward run, bayonets flashing silver in the dawn sun. "Poor shits," he said aloud, as the infantry major who would soon "take a dive" raised his Very pistol high above his head and pulled the trigger. The flare hissed into the sky, trailing white smoke behind it. Crack! It exploded in a burst of bright red. It was the signal the defenders had been waiting for. Suddenly the whole line burst into fire. Rifles cracked, machine guns chattered. The attacking Russians just seemed to melt away. They fell in their tens, their hundreds, arms flailing like puppets

164

in the hands of a crazy puppeteer. But still those behind came on, clambering over the dead and dying bodies of their comrades, shouting like men demented.

Schulze waited no longer. The Russians would be held, but not for long. When the battalion now attacking was wiped out, they would send in another. They seemed to have all the men in the world.

Schulze caught up with the escapers five minutes later. They were working their way along a ditch which ran alongside the dead-straight Kaiserdamm. He nodded his approval. The cheesehead knew what he was about. In the ditch they were relatively safe, for the road itself was littered with dead escapers and refugees who had been caught by Russian artillery or airplanes. He dropped in the ditch and, trying to keep his huge bulk below the level of the road, followed the rest, to find to his surprise that Bormann, of all people, was bringing up the rear.

The portly *Reichsleiter* started suddenly when he became aware that he was being followed, then he recognized the dirty-faced giant and said, "Ah, it's you, Sergeant."

Schulze was tempted to snort, "Who the frig do you think it was – *Winston Churchill*?" But he caught himself in time. Bormann had placed himself in the exposed rear position because he wanted to be away from the two foreign officers. And he could guess why. Bormann did not trust the cheesehead and the *Ami* any longer. He needed him now and the other Wotan troopers. Suddenly Schulze, despite the tough situation, felt quite cheerful. There was going to be money in this for him and the other troopers. "Yes," he told himself happily, as Bormann gave him a wan but friendly smile, "things are beginning to look up at last."

# THREE

A wet, dripping mist hung over the Havel and the surrounding countryside that afternoon when they finally reached it, after a couple of brushes with marauding Cossack cavalry. Now the mist muted the sound of the battle they hoped they had left. But there was something sad, perhaps even eerie, about this new dripping silence. Next to Matz, Heidi shivered uneasily and whispered, "I don't like this place much, Corporal Matz. It's more like winter than spring." She shivered again.

Matz gave her a tired grin. "It's just imagination, Miss," he said reassuringly. "Don't worry. Soon as we find those boats, we'll be off and out of this sh – er – mess," he corrected himself hastily.

"The Führer himself told me that the electric boats were not far from the Kaiserdamm Bridge," Bormann said, his voice low and hushed, as if the sombre mood engendered by the mist-shrouded water had affected him, too. "They can't be far."

Van de Brug didn't answer. His mind was preoccupied with the problem of the big man, Schulze, and his comrades. How were they going to get rid of them once they'd found the boats to make their escape westwards? He knew already that he and Al Kuehn would have to kill them, but the giant sergeant was no fool. He'd be on the lookout all the time. They'd have to catch

166

him off guard and then let him and the others have it.

As they crept forward along the towpath, eyes trying to penetrate the damp, clinging mist, Bormann's mind too was racing feverishly as he considered how he could approach Sergeant Schulze and try to enlist his aid to get rid of the two foreign SS officers. For now he was deadly afraid of them. They were up to no good and he knew it.

Kuehn in the lead, machine pistol at the ready, started to near a line of summer villas close to the bank. They had probably been used before the war by wealthy Berliners who spent their summers out here, away from the noise, the fumes and the heat of the capital, he told himself. Now it seemed they were empty. For it was obvious the first villa he came to had been looted. The door had been smashed in, the windows everywhere were broken, and there was furniture, much of it hacked with what must have been bayonets, strewn everywhere upon what had once been a fine lawn. Now it had been trampled upon by many boots and there were huge ruts where the tanks had gone over it. But below it where the villa had some sort of private mooring there were no signs of the elusive electric boats. He cursed angrily and went on.

Now Bormann saw his chance to contact Sergeant Schulze who was bringing up the rear as usual, routinely turning and peering through the mist to see whether they were being followed. "*Hauptsturm*, I'll go into that house to see if I can find a lavatory to relieve myself."

"Why can't you piss in the open like the rest of us?" Van de Brug said roughly.

"It's not that way."

Van de Brug waved his hand like a schoolmaster might

at a little boy suddenly caught short. "All right, but make it quick. Or we'll go without you."

"Yes immediately. Thank you." Bormann hurried over to the abandoned villa as the rest began to trudge by, pretending to be fumbling with his braces as if he couldn't get to the lavatory quickly enough, but once inside the hall with oils, the canvas slashed, and yellowing photographs of 19th century worthies in high stiff collars peering out from behind shattered glass, he paused and waited tensely for Sergeant Schulze to come by.

There he was, carrying the Schmeisser in his huge paw like a kid's toy, head turning from left in right, systematically studying the ground.

"Sergeant Schulze," he hissed.

Schulze stopped, saw him there and barked, "Yes?"

Bormann held his finger to his lips. "Please – over here."

Schulze shrugged and strolled over, his face puzzled beneath the wet, dripping rim of his helmet. "What is it?" he demanded roughly, looking down at the Party boss.

"I'd like you and your troopers to help me," Bormann said hastily, hoping against hope that van de Brug wouldn't come back to look for him.

"Why – what do you need our help for? You're the big shot. We're only front swine, no-account stubble-hoppers."

Bormann licked his lips nervously. "It's those two SS officers, van de Brug and Kuehn," he hissed. "I think they intend me some harm, I'm certain of it."

Schulze shrugged carelessly. In fact his mind was racing electrically. He'd been right. The fat Party boss was running scared and he wanted the Wotan troopers to help him. "Why should we help you?" he said aloud.

Bormann tapped his chest. "There'll be plenty in it for

you and your good fellows." His fat face was now lathered with sweat and Schulze could see he was almost at the end of his tether.

"What?"

"Money. American dollars. Worth a fortune in Germany these days."

Schulze pretended to consider for a moment. He wasn't going to make it easy for this fat "golden pheasant", who still thought he had a chance in the world even after Germany's defeat. Still the thought of those dollars was very tempting. "What do you want us to do with them if we accept your offer?" he asked cagily.

Bormann smiled up at him. "Disarm them – kill them as far as I am concerned. Renegades like that can never be trusted. They betrayed their own countries and now they are prepared to betray their adopted country. That fool Himmler, a traitor himself too, should never have recruited such trash."

Schulze sniffed and was about to make a sarcastic comment when Kuehn's cry of "there's something up here" made him change his mind.

Bormann looked at him pleadingly. "You will help me, won't you, Sergeant Schulze?"

Schulze was not prepared to let him off the hook just yet. "I'll sleep on it," he growled before turning and doubling over to where the rest of the group had gathered around a crouching Kuehn. "Where's the fire?" he said.

"Shut up," Kuehn hissed, "there's somebody out there, near that end villa." He strained to try to identify the sounds, head turned to one side. To no avail. He bit his bottom lip.

"What do you make of it?" van de Brug asked, peering through the mist, failing to notice Bormann's return.

169

"Hard to say," the American answered. "Might be our people. Could be the Russkis as well, though. But one thing is certain, there are plenty of them. Listen to those voices."

Van de Brug nodded his agreement. For the first time since Schulze had known him, he looked really worried. "It's a bit of a problem to know what to do. Should we try to dodge by or . . ."

"There's somebody in the water," Schulze interrupted him. "I can hear the splashing."

"Perhaps it's the boats we're looking for," Bormann said eagerly and gave the big NCO a pointed look.

Schulze ignored it. "Let's go and have a look," he suggested. "They don't know we're here. We've got the drop on them." His voice was confident and sure and Matz said, "That's the only way. We can't hang around here for ever. We've got to get across the Havel before the Ivans rumble us."

"Yes, you're right," van de Brug agreed. "Let's keep it down to a low roar though, till we find out who they are."

They advanced, bodies bent and tense, weapons at the ready, knowing all of them that they might just well be walking into a trap. But they also knew they had get down the Havel and away before it was too late. There was no alternative.

Now, even though the fog thickened as they got closer to the water, they could hear the voices more clearly and feet splashing in the Havel. Van de Brug held up his hand. They stopped immediately. "I'm sure they're speaking German and they're drinking. Can't you hear the clink of glasses and bottles?"

Kuehn said, "You're right. What the hell's going on? Come on." They crept closer, more puzzled now than apprehensive. What were these people doing carousing when everybody else in Berlin simply wanted to escape from the Russians?

Suddenly the fog parted for a moment or two, a mere window, but big enough for them to see right down to the Havel. Heidi gasped. There were half-naked men everywhere in the water and a few women too. They wore the blue and white shirts of the *Kriegsmarine*, the German Navy, tucked into their belts, and they staggered back and forth through the shallows bearing crates and cases on their shoulders, laughing and giggling drunkenly all the time. Their weapons were thrown casually on the little strip of wet sand. The window opened a little wider for a moment and the watching men could see the source of the supplies: a prewar Havel paddle-steamer sunk in the shallows some ten metres away, her superstructure plastered with holes from shrapnel and pocked with rifle bullets.

Then the window closed once more and they vanished into the fog. Sergeant Schulze whistled softly, "Them blue-boys have certainly laid one on. Stewed as a kite," he said, licking suddenly parched lips at the thought of booze.

"Disgraceful," Bormann snapped. "Drunk and looting. What next?"

"*This*," a harsh voice said behind him.

They turned as one, completely taken by surprise. Forty or so men and a handful of women stood there, their approach deadened by the damp fog. They were dressed in a mixture of Army and Navy uniform, ragged and dirty, but they were all heavily armed, grenades stuck in their belts and boots, bandoliers of cartridges around their shoulders and all of them had their weapons levelled at the surprised escapers.

"All right you sows, get out of my way," the harsh voice

171

boomed. A huge woman with cropped black hair and flashing dark eyes forced her way through the line of men and women and faced the Wotan troopers, feet planted squarely apart like those of a man. Deliberately she threw the stub of a cigar she was smoking to the ground and drew back the grey, ankle-length officer's cloak she was wearing.

They gasped, even Schulze. The huge woman was naked to the waist. Pendulous breasts, tattoed obscenely in blue, with the big nipples painted red, hung down to her broad, iron-buckled man's belt.

She looked at the captives contemptuously. "All right, you bunch of small-balled, soft pricks, drop your weapons."

"But you're German," Bormann objected. "We are, too. Why should we . . ."

"*Halt die Schnauze* – hold your trap," the huge woman interrupted him harshly, "or I'll have the eggs off'n you with a blunt razor." She laughed coarsely and the others laughed with her. "I'm Sarah the Jewess, and this is part of my Free Corps Havel. We owe no loyalty to anyone but ourselves. Now drop those weapons – or else!"

She did not need to complete the threat. The men knew when they were beaten. Miserably they began to drop their weapons, while Sarah the Jewess watched them triumphantly, a look in those dark flashing eyes of hers which boded no good for her new prisoners . . .

# FOUR

The big villa was filled with the men and women of Free Corps Havel. There were all types, soldiers, seamen, airmen and a handful of civilians, plus the women, who mostly looked as tough and as villainous as their male comrades. Men played accordions. Others drank or played the German card game *Skat*, slapping down their cards hard in the traditional fashion. Hard-faced, raddled women danced together cheek on cheek, kissing each other and clapping every time the gramophone record was changed. A sailor was making love to a naked woman on a battered sofa, her bare legs around his neck, while others watched and applauded. A few were delousing themselves, men and women, bare chested, cracking the lice they found in their shirts between their finger nails. It was a scene of chaos, sex and the breakdown of order, save, as Sarah the Jewess passed, that the others showed both fear and respect.

She led them into the inner room. Once obviously it had been the villa's drawing room where the owners had entertained their guests of a Saturday evening with weak German champagne and sweet biscuits, having classy chats about the cosmos and the latest prices on the *Boerse*. Now it was a wreck. The wall tapestries were slashed, the display cabinets broken open and there was a pile of human faeces in the corner.

173

Majestically Sarah the Jewess stalked to the head of a long table and sat herself on a large darkwood high chair that could have doubled for a throne, those pendulous breasts of hers trembling obscenely. Almost immediately, as if she had been waiting behind the door for the huge woman's entrance, a young pretty woman, with dark circles under her eyes, opened it and brought in a tray bearing a gold goblet to offer it to Sarah.

The huge woman chucked her under the chin like a man would do, slapped her pert rump a resounding blow as she turned and cried, raising her goblet in toast. "Here's to a short, fast life." She laughed in a deep bass and downed the goblet's contents in one go. "Gunfire," she gasped, "cognac and frog champagne. There's nothing to beat it." She wiped her lips with the back of a dirty paw. "All right, let me tell you where you've landed yourselves." Her voice was very businesslike now.

They waited.

She grinned at them evilly. "We're rats, to put it simply. Deserters, escapees from concentration camps like me, black marketeers, pimps, whores, ladies with special tastes which don't include men." She looked down in mock modesty and Schulze told himself, "Christ, she's one of those." He pressed closer to Heidi and thanked God she was as dirty and ragged as they were, looking the part of a hairy-assed stubble-hopper. "In other words a fair cross-section of our noble German people."

She let the words sink in before continuing. "So what are we going to do?" She answered her own question with a laconic "*Survive*, that's what. We're going to let no one and nothing stand in our way. Anybody tries and he, or she, is a dead 'un." She drew a dirty forefinger under her chin, as if slitting a throat, to make her meaning quite clear.

"We loot. There's still plenty of stuff to loot around here. There's the Havel crossing too for those shits who are trying to do a bunk." Matz looked significantly at Schulze. He nodded back. So the big Lesbian had the electric boats. "Plenty of loot in that as well. Finally when the Russkis are through, we'll have the whole of one of the richest capitals in Europe to loot at our pleasure." She threw out her hairy arms expansively and those monstrous dugs if hers trembled like puddings.

Her eyes narrowed and she leaned forward from her throne, evil eyes narrowed to slits. "What do you say? Want to throw in your lot with us, eh?"

There was no response. The woman's face grew angry. "Well, come on, spit it out. *Quick. Dalli . . . dalli!*"

It was Schulze who saved the day, while all around his comrades were too dazed to react and Bormann trembled with sheer unadulerated fear. "Of course we will. What have we to lose? We can't get across the Havel, we haven't got any boats. Sure, we're with you." He gave a broad grin.

The huge woman looked hard at Schulze, as if seeing him for the first time, sizing him up and apparently liking what she saw. "Come here," she said, crooking a big finger at him.

Schulze pushed his way through the rest to where the woman sat. She reached out a hand and gripped his shoulder. Even Schulze winced at the grip. "You've got a good pair of shoulders on you," she grunted and then before he could react, she had grabbed his flies. "Hey!" he cried startled, as she felt his testicles, more gently, however, than she had his shoulder. "Yes," she concluded, "you've got plenty in the trousers." She released her hold and Schulze swallowed hard. What the devil was the woman up to?

175

But before he could find out, the girl who had brought the goblet in thrust her head round the door and said urgently, "Sarah, *Russians*! It's the gunship again."

Sarah forgot Schulze and what she had in mind for him. Hastily she rose and strode to the window, shouting over her shoulder as she did so, "Tell those rats to get down out of sight and shut up. You lot, you do the same!"

"Yes Sarah." The girl fled.

Hastily the men of Wotan dropped to the dirty littered floor, as the huge woman peered out of the window from behind the curtain. Schulze to her right risked a peek too. A small boat, its high, old-fashioned funnel emitting thick black smoke, was puffing its way across the waterway, its decks lined with heavily armed Red Army men. Sarah saw him looking and whispered, "Former Havel pleasure steamer. The Ivans took it over last week. Now they patrol the Havel in it, looking for escapees and the like. They sank that one we were looting yesterday evening. But the fog came down and the blue boys managed to beach it."

"Do you think they've come back to check?" Schulze asked, as the gunboat vanished into the mist for a moment or two.

"We'll see. We'd tackle them ourselves, but they've got a 57mm gun on board – they've fixed it up on the deck somehow or other – and we can't manage that . . ." She stopped short. The gunboat had changed course and was chuffing and puffing directly for the beached paddle-steamer. "Shit!" she cursed.

With surprising speed for a woman so big, she crossed the room and called through the door, "All right, you rogues and cut-throats, stand by. It looks as if the Ivans are heading our way." Everywhere the men and women scrambled for their weapons frantically, even the naked girl who had just been copulating on the sofa. Sarah looked at the Wotan troopers. "You, too, now you're with us. You know what's going to happen to you if you fall into the hands of the Ivans, especially you SS officers." She looked pointedly at an ashen-faced, trembling Bormann, and laughed harshly. "They'll have the balls off'n yer with a blunt razor-blade." Bormann went even paler.

Schulze and Matz grabbed their weapons from the big table and with Heidi between them crouched beneath the window, watching the boat approach, moving at almost a snail's pace through the mist. "Listen the two of you," Schulze whispered, knowing that the woman was concentrating on the approaching craft as well, "we've got to get out of this den of thieves as soon as we can. This very night if we can manage it."

Urgently Matz nodded his agreement. "Yes, there's no future here for us."

"And we're taking Bormann with us – *for a while*. He's got money, foreign money, and we're going to need that kind of cabbage when we get to the West."

"The officers?" Matz snapped quickly, as the gunboat stopped and a Russian clambered up to the roof of the bridge to attempt to pierce the mist with his binoculars.

Schulze made a clicking gesture with his big forefinger. "That, if we have to," he whispered grimly, "there are no two ways about it."

"Agreed," Matz said as the gunboat's engine started up again and the man on top of the bridge clambered down hurriedly. Presumably he had not been able to spot the beached paddle-steamer in the mist. It started to move away.

"Relax," Sarah the Jewess said in that tough manner of hers, "we live to fight another day – or is it fuck?" She chuckled and relit the stump of her cigar.

There were sighs, grunts. Someone farted. Their every gesture indicated that this had been a close one.

"All right," Sarah the Jewess said, "you can put down your weapons and help to unload the rest of the loot from the steamer. Then we'll shove it out into the deeper water and sink it. Perhaps then we'll have peace with that gunboat."

Van de Brug and Kuehn looked for a moment as if they might refuse, but changed their minds. They started to file out with the rest. Schulze slung his Schmeisser and was preparing to join then when the woman commanded, "No, not you." He turned and looked at her and she added, "I've got something else for a big ox like you."

Schulze shot her a hard look, then said, as if resigned to whatever she had in mind for him, "Crap, said the King and a thousand arseholes bent and took the strain for in those days the word of the King was law."

She grinned. "That's the style, big boy. That's the style! Come along with me. I want you to meet someone who is very special to me. This way."

Imperiously she strode through the crowded villa, head held high, breasts swinging and jiggling under the long cloak. She paused at a door at the far end of the big hall and to Schulze's complete surprise, she knocked on it.

"Come in," a soft, very feminine voice called.

Sarah the Jewess touched her hair quickly to ensure it was in place, then she swept in, a sudden, sweet smile on her broad face. Over her shoulder Schulze caught a glimpse of a young blonde, with smouldering bedroom eyes, a mocking sensual mouth, painted a bright scarlet, but with a livid weal of a vicious knife scar running down the left side of her pretty oval face.

Behind him Schulze heard one of the drunks, who was looking, too, through the open door, whisper hoarsely, "That one is like a kid, a silly perverted kid. She wants anything handsome she sees in pants, and that great mare of a Jewess sees she gets what she wants. The lesbian's crazy about her."

"Little Dora," Sarah the Jewess cooed, "I've brought someone – for tonight. I hope he's all right? He's well endowed. I've felt." She stepped to one side to reveal Schulze, red-faced and for once in his life actually embarrassed, for he felt at that moment like a stud bull.

The young blonde mustered him for a long moment, then she announced, licking her scarlet, wet lips, "He'll do. He'll be my prick for this night."

# FIVE

The Wotan troopers huddled apart from the drunken Free Corps men and their women. It was late afternoon and they were eating hunks of black bread and cold bacon, washed down with beer – Schulze had warned them previously that there was going to be none of the "hard stuff". This night he wanted them sober.

"I'm supposed to fuck her," he announced baldly, "if you'll pardon my French, *Fraulein*."

"But I thought she was the big Jewess's little playmate?" Matz objected,

"She is, but she likes men as well," Schulze replied, "and the big Yiddess is crazy about her. She does everything that little bit of beaver wants. So I've been selected to dance the mattress polka with her tonight."

Matz sniffed. "Can't be all that bad," he opined. "Personally I've got so much ink in my fountain pen I don't know who to write to first."

Schulze ignored the remark. "Well, I'm going to let them think I'm playing ball with them, lull them into a false sense of security." He lowered his voice. "But this night we're going out and taking his nibs" – he nodded to where Bormann sat with the two SS officers in the midst of the drinking mob of pimps, prostitutes and deserters looking distinctly unhappy – "with us."

180

"But we don't have no boats," one of the Wotah troopers objected.

"No, but I know where to get some," Schulze answered. "They've got them hidden in those bushes and reeds beyond the curve in the bank. They're the electric ones as well."

Heidi's wan, dirty face, still smeared with grease to hide her identity, lit up. "Then we'll be able to get out of this awful place." Hastily she took her eyes off a drunken whore, who had lifted her skirts and was urinating standing up like a man.

Matz patted her hand reassuringly. "There, there," he said like a doting mother. "Everything's going to be all right."

"That's enough of that, *Granny*," Schulze snapped. "Now pin back yer spoons and listen to what I have to say. As soon as I go in there to – er – perform, you, Matz, and Heidi will go outside – find some excuse – and get to those boats. They might have a guard on them, but I doubt it with this shower of shit." He looked across at one of the drunks, a villainous-looking creature who looked as if he hadn't shaved for a week, who was showing off to his equally drunken comrades by eating pieces of a broken razor-blade. "You, Mannemann, and Hatz, get Bormann away from the cheesehead and the *Ami*. Try to do it without force if you can." The two troopers nodded their understanding. "The rest of you will cover him with whatever force you might have to use till you get to the boats . . ."

"And you, brave Sergeant Schulze?" Heidi cut in, her voice full of concern. "What about you?"

Schulze was moved, but he wasn't about to show that to her. "Don't worry about me, Heidi. I can take care of myself. If I can't cope with a nympho and a lezzie," he shrugged, "I might as well up my toes and make a handsome stiff, here and now."

"Don't say that," she protested and pressed his big steam shovel of a paw. "You know we all worry about you."

"Oh, my holy shitting Christ!" Matz moaned. "I think I'm going to have my monthlies." He gave what he thought was a falsetto female moan . . .

Sarah the Jewess's face glowed with anticipation as she poured the last jug of hot water into "little Dora's" bath. The towels and the perfume, plus powder, she used on her were already in place. "Everything's ready," she said finally. "First the massage."

Little Dora yawned, as if very bored. She popped a last chocolate into her scarlet-lipped mouth and spread herself out on the table. "If you must," she said.

Sarah swallowed hard. Then she placed her big hands on her mistress's delightful young body, drinking it in in all its splendid nakedness. With all her skill she kneaded little Dora's breasts, running her paws up and down the length of the girl's slighty spread legs, feeling herself beginning to pant with desire. Little Dora didn't seem to notice. She reached over to the box of looted chocolates and popped another *praline* into her cunning little mouth.

Sarah the Jewess sighed. Why could she never satisfy the little, delightful beast? Others, men and women, were desperately afraid of her. Not Dora.

She rolled her lover over and began massaging her back, taking a sad kind of pleasure at the firm, pert young buttocks. Lovingly she rubbed the back down to the buttocks and then planting a kiss on each one, she stopped and said, "Must you?"

Dora turned, selected another chocolate and chewing it slowly, asked, "What?"

"You know. Tonight, with that big hunk."

Dora looked at her coldly. "Do you wish to spoil one of my few pleasures?" she asked haughtily. "I give you what you want, don't I?"

Sarah the Jewess hung her head. "I am sorry, Little Dora," she whispered.

"Speak up!"

"I'm very sorry, Little Dora."

"Then that's an end to it. My bath."

Effortlessly the big lesbian gathered Little Dora up in her brawny arms. Slowly she deposited the naked blonde in the fragant hot water and began soaping her while Little Dora helped herself to another chocolate, as if she were totally unaware of the other woman.

Sadly, but still enjoying herself, Sarah the Jewess rubbed the thick fragant suds over her mistress's breasts and wondered again about the hold Little Dora seemed to have on her. For her part, Little Dora chewed her chocolate and thought of nothing . . .

Now all was silent in the big villa. Drunken men and women sprawled everywhere, surrounded by broken glasses, empty bottles and, here and there, vomit. Now the only sound was the faint hiss of the wind in the trees outside and hefty snoring from the far end of the big dining room where a drunken sailor slept on the table, wrapped up in a thick velvet curtain. Almost noiselessly for such a huge woman, Sarah the Jewess crossed the floor to where the Wotan men lay. She touched Schulze's arm. "Come now," she whispered.

Schulze, who had been feigning sleep, waiting for this moment, as had the other Wotan troopers, pretended to wake up with difficulty. Then finally he got to his feet, rubbed his eyes and grumbled, "God what a frigging life!"

"Don't waste time," the big woman ordered sternly. "She wants you now and whatever Little Dora wants, she gets – *or else!*"

"Oh don't go on about it," Schulze said and as he passed Matz, he gave his good foot a kick just to make sure he hadn't really gone to sleep. But Matz wasn't asleep. He knew, as did the rest, that if they didn't get away this night, they never would. They'd die in Berlin.

A knife of yellow light slid into the dark room momentarily, as the door to Little Dora's room was opened. Then it closed and everything was darkness once more. "Thalmann," Matz whispered to the big Wotan trooper lying on the floor next to him. "Me and the Miss are off. You're in charge of the rest. Keep yer glassy orbits peeled . . ."

"Like tinned tomatoes," Thalmann answered cheerfully, using the old phrase.

"*Los*," Matz whispered.

Heidi rose obediently and noiselessly, for both of them had pulled socks over their boots. They crossed the room to the rear entrance to the villa. Nobody stirred. They opened and closed the door silently. Heidi shivered in the coldness of the night air after the fug inside the villa.

"Don't be scared," Matz whispered.

"I'm not scared, Corporal Matz," the girl hissed. "Especially not with you and Sergeant Schulze."

Matz shook his head in mock wonder. *Fraulein* Heidi obviously thought the sun shone out of his and Schulze's arseholes. That made him feel old. She'd be calling him "uncle" next. "Come on," he whispered, "let's go and see if we can secure those boats." They disappeared into the darkness.

Kuehn stirred uneasily. He was unable to sleep. The stink of stale tobacco and beer nauseated him. Besides, his mind was racing electrically. Here he was lying next to Bormann, who represented a fortune, freedom and a life of luxury in some banana republic, probably for the rest of his days, and he couldn't do anything about it due to the big Yid and her pack of cut-throats. It was absolutely maddening.

To his left van de Brug whispered, "Can't you sleep?"

"No."

"Me neither." He crept closer to the American so that his mouth was close to the other man's ear. "He could do a bunk tonight, you know," he hissed.

"I know. But would the office stallion," he meant Bormann, "come with us?"

"You think he's on to us?"

"Yes," Kuehn answered. He looked up. Through the window a thin beam of spectral silver light had appeared. Beyond he could see the sickle moon. It would be just light enough to see without blundering into anything and awaking the rat pack, but dark enough to cover their flight. "We could make him come with us," he said tentatively.

Van de Brug didn't answer for a moment or two, as if he were considering the matter seriously. "But he might kick up a racket," he said then.

The two fell silent again, as they thought about it. At their side Bormann had begun to snore. Outside, Kuehn thought he heard soft steps, but he dismissed the idea that there was anyone out there. "These drunken rats," he told himself, "don't even post sentries." Though that was to their advantage this night, if they could only get Bormann outside without rousing the others.

"What about this?" van de Brug whispered. "The fat

pig has been guzzling beer all evening. Sooner or later he'll have to go outside to piss. You know the state of the thunderboxes in here. So he'll go out, then we'll nobble him. What do you think?"

"Well, it's a bit chancy," Kuehn said after a moment. "But I can't think of anything better. So for the time being let's hope that works. But," he added, voice determined and hard, "one way or other we've got to get him out before dawn. And tonight is our last chance. March or croak, Piet."

"March or croak, Al."

Both of them lay back and placing their hands beneath their heads stared at the dirty, peeling ceiling like men who had too much on their consciences to allow them to sleep . . .

# SIX

Little Dora lay on an enormous bed covered by a clean white sheet, clad only in skimpy sheer black silk knickers. As always she was eating chocolates, popping them into that sensuous scarlet mouth of hers, one after another. "The stallion," Sarah the Jewess said grumpily. She pushed Schulze forward.

Little Dora waved her hand in dismissal, not taking her gaze off Schulze, who suddenly felt awkward and out of place. He had never experienced a situation like this before. He'd always taken the woman; now it was the other way around. Reluctantly the big lesbian went out and closed the door behind her.

"Schnapps," Little Dora commanded. "Pour me a glass. Have one yourself. Put some fire in your blood." She indicated the stone bottle on the table next to the solitary candle burning under a red glass shade, casting a warm exotic glow over the bedroom.

Schulze didn't need to be told twice. A shot was exactly what he needed at this particular moment. He poured her a glass and she held out her hand for it, as if she had been accustomed to have been waited on by servants all her life. Then, while she sipped hers slowly, looking over the rim of the water glass with those seductive bedroom eyes of hers, he poured himself a glass and took a good slug of it. The schnapps hit the back of his throat, went down with a gurgle and then almost immediately he could feel the new fire flood his body.

"Take your uniform off," Little Dora said suddenly.

"Everything?"

"Except your boots. I like to feel men's boots on my body. I don't know why, but I do."

Schulze drained the rest of his schnapps in one go and started to pull off his tunic and shirt. She followed his every move, drinking in the sight of those brawny, hairy arms, the powerful ribcage scarred here and there with old bullet wounds.

"You stink of man," she hissed. "Sweat and earth and man . . ." She stopped short. He had dropped his breeches and underpants, clambering out of them hastily.

She swallowed hard and reaching out her free hand, she cradled his sexual organs, as if she were weighing them. "The Jewess was right. You are a well-hung stallion."

She closed her eyes and quivered with desire. "My breasts," she said thickly. "Put your big paws on my tits – *now!*"

His thick fingers ground into her breasts. Immediately her large, dun-coloured nipples sprang up with excitement and her mouth opened with passion. She sighed. He squeezed harder. Her spine arched and her head fell backwards.

Suddenly Schulze felt himself in charge. "Touch it," he commanded. "At once!"

Blindly she ran her hand across his black-matted, muscular chest. For a moment or two she allowed herself the sensual pleasure of feeling hairy, steel-hard muscle. Then her hand dropped lower and lower. He bent his head over her and began to suck her nipples. He moved from one to the other, sucking and kissing, kissing and sucking.

188

Her breath was coming in sharp little gasps. Her fingers found and touched that which she sought. She choked with surprised pleasure. It seemed she had never felt such a great column of hard flesh before.

"Yes," Schulze said happily, moving his lips from her breasts, "you don't often get a diamond cutter like that, girl."

She didn't reply; she couldn't. She was too thrilled by what she touched. Greedily she ran her fingers through his pubic hair and felt the weight of the massive balls hanging below. "Oh my God," she groaned. "Oh, my God!"

Schulze bit her left nipple. Her body jerked with delight. Automatically she tightened her grip upon him, giving him a shudder of pain-pleasure. "Watch them balls," he warned. "They're the only pair I've got, girl."

But Little Dora was no longer listening. She was wrapped totally in her own pleasure, as she fondled him cunningly with her delicate little fingers which were now wet with sweat.

Schulze grinned triumphantly. He had her now, he knew, as he listened to her excited sighing shudders of intense delight.

But even as he played with her, his mind was working on how he was going to turn this night to his advantage. He guessed the big lesbian would not be asleep yet. She would be guarding over her lover somewhere out there until Little Dora was finished with them. Then would be the time to make a run for it. No sentries and the gang's female chief asleep. But he couldn't spend all night with the little nympho. They had to be out and have crossed the Havel before dawn. "Screw her to sleep, Schulzi," a hard little voice at the back of his brain rasped. "Give her the works. Anyway it's fun, ain't it?"

He nodded his agreement, sweat already breaking out

over his naked body. He knocked away her importuning hands and snapped, "Take it in your mouth, girl."

Surprisingly enough for a girl who wielded so much power in the cut-throats' camp she did. Her mouth was like a furnace and her naked body was glazed with sweat in the ruddy glow cast by the candle, as she licked and sucked him. Schulze forced himself not to feel pleasure. He wanted to wear her out. He had to keep control of himself. He couldn't finish too soon. For a few moments he allowed her to continue, then he barked roughly, "Enough of that. Off with those drawers."

Sobbing with excitement, she pulled off the black silk knickers eagerly. "What now?" she gasped as she eyed his erection standing out like a policeman's club.

"What do you think?" he sneered. "Spread 'em!"

"Yes . . . yes . . . at once," she choked, her voice shaky and strangled. Hurriedly she spread her slim white legs to reveal the pink line of wet flesh among the black hair.

He grabbed a pillow and thrust it roughly under her buttocks. "I want you to get all that's coming to you," he growled threateningly. "You're going to have to take it all."

"Oh, my God," she quavered, eyes wild and mad with excitement, the sweat glazing her face, as if her features had been rubbed in vaseline. "*Oh, my God!*"

He thrust into the girl's loins. She wimpered with pain and pleasure. "I've never . . ."

"Shut up!" he snapped and slapped her across the face, as if he were carried away by a great sexual passion and didn't want to be disturbed in his overwhelming animal lust. In reality, he was cool as a cucumber, giving a performance as he had never done before.

For the next half-hour he played with her body. Like some monstrous human hammer he rose and fell upon

190

her in the ruddy light of the trembling candle so that her whole sweat-lathered body trembled violently under each stroke and she whimpered with pain and pleasure. More than once she climaxed and cried, "I'm exhausted." But he had no mercy. He lifted her clean off the sweat-soaked rumpled bed and spiked her on top of him savagely.

She screamed. "*It's too much!*" He showed no mercy. He pumped himself into her mechanically, knowing that he could go on for hours without climaxing now. He was fully in control of himself. She responded with thick snorts of sheer ecstasy. With ever wilder strokes, her heart thumping crazily, as if it might break out of her ribcage at any moment from an overwhelming sexual excitement, she pumped herself up and down on that majestic column of flesh which seemed to fill her whole body. Great hysterical gurgling moans came from her throat, as he thrust himself savagely between her taut dripping haunches. She sobbed, she cried, she muttered unintelligible words. Then there it was. "*Fuck . . . fuck . . . fuck . . . oh, fuck!*" she cried, skinny body wet with sweat. She screamed and went limp in his hands, head hanging to one side as if she were dead.

Quite gently for such a big rough man, Schulze lowered her to the bed. She was fast asleep before he covered her with the wet sheet. On the other side of the door, Sarah the Jewess shook her head sadly, the tears streaming down her hard, raddled face. Slowly she started to make her way to her own lonely bed.

Schulze waited. He had heard the other woman go away. All was silent once more, save for the muted snoring coming from the other room. His hands trembling slightly, he picked up the schnapps bottle and took a hefty slug straight from the neck. Then he raised it as if in toast to the sleeping blonde and whispered, "You're a

191

good fuck, Little Dora, I'll say that for you." Then he took another slug of the fiery schnapps, the exhausted sleeping woman forgotten already.

Silently he slipped back into his uniform. Little Dora slept on. Schulze shook his head in mock wonder as he buttoned up his shabby tunic. What a crazy world it was – Berlin this May! What was he doing fucking the bisexual mistress of a Jewish cut-throat gang leader against a background of a dying Berlin, while trying to rescue – only for his money naturally – a fleeing top Nazi Party boss? "Nuts," he whispered to himself, "absolutely nuts." He buckled up his pistol belt and dismissed the matter. It didn't do any good, he told himself, to consider such matters. To survive this May you had to take life as it came and not try to find some deeper meaning to it.

Softly he tiptoed to the door. He opened it carefully and stopped dead. A portly figure he recognized immediately had risen from the ranks of the sleeping men and women and was beginning to thread his way through the bodies everywhere on the floor. It was Bormann, and Schulze, his heart racing suddenly, could guess where he was going. He had been drinking beer all evening. Now he was going outside to urinate.

But as he stood there in the shadows, he could see Bormann was not going outside alone. Two other figures had risen carefully and were beginning to follow the Party boss. "The cheesehead and the *Ami*," he told himself. They were not going to let their meal ticket for the future out of their eyes. Or – he bit his bottom lip thoughtfully. He realized the two of them must have been awake all along. They were not just accompanying Bormann on his piss just in case he tried to do a bunk. How could he? The Party boss needed someone else to take care of him. On his own he would be sunk. No, van de Brug and

192

Kuehn had the same idea as he had: they were going to spirit Bormann away under the cover of darkness. The time had come for the showdown, the final confrontation between what was left of the Wotan troopers and the two SS officers.

Schulze hesitated no longer. As the two of them followed Bormann to the outside, he stole over to where the Wotan men lay on the floor. Mannemann was awake, though the rest slept. He sat up immediately, tough face looking worried in the shaft of silver shining coldly through the window. "Yes, I saw them go," he said before Schulze could speak. "But I didn't know what to do, Schulze."

"It's all right. Anything you might have done would have woken this bunch of rats and we would have had them on our necks as well. Come on," he added hastily, "let's get these sleeping beauties on their feet. We haven't got any time to lose . . ."

# SEVEN

In the fashion of an old soldier, Matz smoked with the glowing end of his cigarette tucked in his hollowed hand so as not to give away his position. At his feet, sitting on the deck of the nearest of the electric boats, Heidi shivered a little in the cold and whispered, "Do you think they'll be long, Corporal Matz? It is cold out here on the water." She looked at the water, a shining silver in the sickle moon.

Matz thought his of old running mate ramming it into Little Dora and considered whether he should tell Heidi that "dear Sergeant Schulze" could make quite a pig of himself when it came to gash. He decided, however, not to tell her of such *Schweinereien*. Instead he said, "No, once he's done his – er – duty, he'll soon be here. We'll be across by dawn and on our way westwards."

"I hope so," Heidi sighed a little wanly. "I made a fool of myself in the bunker. It was the alcohol . . ." She hung her head momentarily. "Oh how glad I'll be go to the West. My mother lives in Brunswick, that's in the American zone. I'll be safe there. I never want to see Berlin ever again."

"You can say that again," Matz agreed heartily. He took one last puff at the cigarette and then put out the glowing end on the heel of his boot.

"What will you do, Corporal Matz?" she asked. "Have you got a family to go to, now the war's over?"

Corporal Matz had started several families in half a dozen European countries since 1939, more than he cared to remember. All the same he shook his head. "No time for families. I've spent the last six years at the front, fighting."

She reached out and touched his hand gently. "Poor Corporal Matz. But I'm sure now you'll find a good woman who'll make you a fine wife and give you children."

The words shocked Matz. He didn't particularly want a good woman – he preferred bad ones. As for kids, all they were good for was to have grub stuck down their necks which they immediately shot out of the other end. But what was he going to do now that it was all virtually over? All he'd ever known was SS Assault Regiment Wotan and the war. Christ, it was frightening!

Suddenly Heidi turned her head to one side. "There's somebody coming," she announced after a moment of listening hard. "I can just hear footsteps."

"It'll be Schulze and the boys," Matz said eagerly and straightened up. "We're on our way . . ." He stopped short. It was Kuehn. There was no mistaking the big American as he came down the path, Schmeisser already levelled, its muzzle pointing straight at the two of them. "All right," he snapped. "No funny tricks. Drop your weapons, the two of you. Come on. Quick." He jerked up the muzzle threateningly.

Miserably Matz unbuckled his Schmeisser and dropped it to the ground. Heidi did the same awkwardly, looking at him enquiringly, as if she expected him to give her some kind of explanation for this sudden change of events.

Van de Brug came into view, pushing a sullen and

frightened Bormann in front of him. "All right, you two, release the first boat and start it up."

Kuehn nodded his agreement as he covered them.

Miserably the two prisoners began to carry out the Dutchman's orders under Kuehn's watchful gaze.

Matz balanced himself on the swaying little deck. He turned on the power switch. The controls, which were simple, glowed a sudden green. He looked for the starter button. The thing was really a glorified canoe powered by electric batteries. He imagined the things had been used by courting couples and the like in peacetime. For a moment he pondered grabbing Heidi and getting underway with her. Then he looked at the speedometer, and decided against it. The top speed was only ten kilometres an hour. They'd both be dead ducks before they'd gone five metres. Miserably he pressed the starter. With a soft, almost inaudible hum, the motor started at once.

Kuehn said, "All right, Piet, drag him aboard now. You two," he meant Matz and Heidi, "get out of the way. *Dalli.*"

Reluctantly Matz clambered out of the little boat and moved over to where Heidi was standing, head bent so that Bormann couldn't recognize her. For a moment the little corporal thought Kuehn was going to shoot them. Then he realised that that would wake up the Jewess's cut-throats. They wouldn't want that.

"Right, if you know what's good for you," Kuehn snapped, "you'll keep your traps shut until we're way over to the middle." With his right foot, he kicked the two Schmeissers into the water. "Remember, any funny business and I can gun you down from the boat up to a range of sixty metres. Got it?"

"Got it," Matz muttered unhappily, his mind racing as

196

he wondered what to do next, but his brain seemed blank. He couldn't think of anything.

Van de Brug pushed Bormann into the boat. He and then Kuehn followed, with the latter sitting in the stern, Schmeisser levelled at the two persons standing miserably on the bank.

Van de Brug pushed open the little throttle. Virtually noiselessly, the little craft started to pull away slowly. Helplessly the two of them watched as it drew away at a steady five kilometres an hour. At the stern Kuehn relaxed, lowering the muzzle of his Schmeisser, knowing now that they had done it. They had their passport to the future. In high good humour, he waved to Matz and Heidi, saying in English, "So long, suckers!"

It was just then that Schulze at the head of the other Wotan troopers came panting up the towpath. He took in the scene at once. "Why, the shits have stolen the boat!" Next to him Mannemann raised his rifle. Schulze knocked the muzzle down swiftly. "Are you crazy, man? We don't want to wake that mob in there. *Los*, don't all stand there like farts in a trance. Into the other two boats. It's gonna be a tight squeeze, but we can manage it. Come on."

Frantically they slashed through the hawsers with their bayonets, while Matz sprang from the one boat to the other, starting up the electric motors as he had done for the SS officers. Slowly the packed craft began to draw away from the bank. But each boat was carrying twice the load of the other craft and try as they may they could not get their boats to go any faster than five knots. Slowly but surely the craft steered by van de Brug began to draw away from them, growing ever smaller as it skimmed across the silver water.

Schulze raged inwardly. But he knew he could do nothing but keep up the chase. As long as he could see the other craft and spot where the three men went ashore, the men of Wotan still stood a chance. Once they lost sight of their quarry, then they'd be out of luck. "Scout around, lads," he called, "see if there's anything we can chuck overboard and lighten the load."

"What about you?" Matz suggested, trying to relieve the tension, but Schulze was in no mood for jokes. "Knock it off, wisearse," he snarled.

There were a few things – a couple of boxes, a can containing lubrication oil and crates of rations – that they were able to toss over the side. But the speed of the two little craft didn't increase to any degree. They were simply overladen with men. Still they kept on in the wake of their quarry doggedly, the men straining their eyes in the cold silver gloom to keep the other craft in view.

Ten minutes passed. Behind them on the bank of the Havel, firing broke out suddenly. Schulze swung round, startled. "Heaven, arse and cloudburst!" he swore wildly. "What do those birdbrains think they are about?"

There were scores of tiny figures running along the towpath, firing wildly as they did so and, by cocking his head to one side, Schulze could just catch their shouts and cries of anger. "That Yid has her head between her frigging legs," he said angrily. "Don't she know that'll bring the frigging Popovs on the scene? You can hear that racket all the way to the Führerbunker!"

How right he was, Sergeant Schulze would soon learn. But now he willed the little craft to catch up with van de Brug's boat which now was a mere speck against the silver lake of water. But still his boat continued to plod on at a mere five kilometres an hour. The race, he told himself sadly, had virtually been lost . . .

\*      \*      \*

198

"What are you going to do with me?" Bormann demanded. Inwardly he was trembling with fear. But outwardly he put on a bold face, trying to overawe the two kidnappers, for that was what they were – he knew that – with a show of his old authority.

Van de Brug laughed easily. "What do you think, *Reichsleiter*?" He emphasized the grandiose title cynically.

"You wish to rob me?"

"Of course," van de Brug said, complete master of the situation.

"Then take the money once we reach the far shore and let me go," Bormann said, reasoning he still had a small fortune in bullion in Sweden, once he reached that neutral country.

"I'm afraid not," the Dutchman said.

"Definitely not," Kuehn agreed, shaking his head. "You're our hostage to fortune, Bormann."

"What is that supposed to mean, man?" Bormann blustered, his confidence draining away fast.

"It means," Kuehn said slowly, tapping out each word with his forefinger on Bormann's fat chest, as if he were driving home yet another nail in the *Reichsleiter*'s coffin, "after we've taken your loot, we're going deliver you to the British up in the north. Do you think they'd bother about letting a couple of junior SS officers go free when they've got Number Three in the Third Reich in their hands?" Kuehn smiled coldly. "I don't . . ." The words froze on his lips. "Oh, my frigging God!" he exclaimed.

"What is it?" van de Brug asked in sudden alarm.

Kuehn pointed to the east with a finger that trembled badly. "It's the gunboat, that same damn Russki gunboat from yesterday. And it's heading straight for us. *Fuck!*"

# EIGHT

*Crump!* Scarlet flame stabbed the silver gloom. From the bow of the gunboat a solid whirling white blob came speeding towards the electric boat.

"Holy cow!" Kuehn exclaimed in English, "They're firing solid AP* at us!"

At the wheel, van de Brug swung the little craft desperately. It seemed to take an age to turn. With a great whoosh like an express racing through a station, the 57mm shell flashed by them to plunge into the water fifty yards on.

"My God . . . my God," Bormann quavered, holding his hands to his face like women do in moments of fear, "this is the end!"

"Hold yer goddamn water," Kuehn snarled and, raising his machine pistol, loosed off a long burst at the approaching gunboat. He knew it was too far away for him to hit, but it soothed his jingling nerves to be able to do something.

Again the gunboat fired. Another white blurr hurried towards them, trailing fiery red sparks behind it. With a great splash, it sent up a fountain of whirling white water fifty yards to their front. "They're ranging in!" van de Brug yelled above the roar of the gunboat's engines, as it closed

---

* Armour-piercing.

rapidly with the little boat. Wildly he flung a glance about it. Now in the silver moonlight he could just see the dark smudge of the opposite bank. It was about a hundred or so metres away.

Kuehn took in his glance. "Keep going as long as possible in the boat," he yelled, "and then we swim for it."

"I can't swim," Bormann shrieked.

"Then fucking well drown!" Kuehn yelled back.

"We'll help you," van de Brug cried, keeping his head, knowing just how important Bormann was for the two of them. Again he forced the little boat into a new turn, trying to put the enemy gunners off. But even as he did so he knew their luck wouldn't hold out much longer. It could be only a matter of minutes now.

From about two hundred metres away, Schulze and the rest of the Wotan troopers watched the unequal battle. They had throttled back and were hardly moving at all in the hope that they would keep out of the range of the Russian gunboat but they could see the flash of the craft's gun and every time its shells came hurtling through the night they could spot their quarry outlined a stark black against the incandescent bright white of the AP shells.

"They'll abandon the boat in half a mo," Schulze said. "They'll try to swim ashore. If we can manage to keep out of trouble till they reach it I think we've got 'em."

"Agreed," Matz said, as the gun fired once again and another shell came scurrying lethally through the night. "They'll have a go at hiding out till the Ivans have gone. If they make it," he added.

"Yer, if they make it . . ." His words were drowned by the sound of a shell striking home. In a sudden vivid flash of light they could see the bow of the little electric boat rear up in the air. Next moment it disintegrated in a mess of flying wood and metal, great blue electric sparks from the motors zig-zagging crazily into the night sky.

"Great crap on the Christmas tree!" Schulze shouted above the roar of the exploding boat. "They've bought it!"

"No, they haven't," Matz yelled back. "Look."

A searchlight had snapped on in the bow of the gunboat. Now its hard white beam searched the water, while a machine gunner sprayed its surface with tracer.

"They must have jumped over the side just in time, Schulze," he cried. "Why would they be shooting at the water otherwise?"

Schulze said nothing.

For a moment the men in the two other electric boats watched as the Russians systematically swept the surface of the water with their machine gun. Then the searchlight clicked off, leaving them suddenly blinking and trying to focus their eyes in the abrupt gloom. The firing stopped and then the boat gathered speed, heading for the shore behind them.

"It's obvious they're off to see what that firing was," Matz said. "That Yid and her queer girlfriend are in for trouble – that's my guess anyhow."

Again Schulze said nothing, as the gunboat grew ever smaller.

"Penny for 'em," Matz snapped.

"I was just thinking," Schulze said slowly.

"Oh, that's it then. I thought you were pissing in the wind."

Schulze wasn't offended. "I was just thinking did they buy it or did they get away with it? You know that cheesehead and the *Ami* are cunning arseholes. They might just well have pulled it off and then they'll be out, hiding in the bushes with Bormann *and* the money." His voice grew stronger. "And I'd hate for them to get away with it."

"Well, there's only one way for us to find out," Matz said.

"Yes, I know, Come on, lads. Let's go and have a look-see." Slowly the two little crafts started to gather speed.

Bormann gasped and choked, as Kuehn pumped his arms up and down as he lay there on the ground, forcing the water from his lungs, saying, "It's all right. You're not going to die *yet*." The American stopped his pumping, satisfied that the Party boss would be all right now. He turned to van de Brug who, with his wooden arm, had had a tough time of it swimming that last desperate hundred metres. "You OK, Piet?" he asked in English.

Van de Brug swallowed hard and fought to control his hectic breathing. "Sure, Al," he said thickly. "Just give me a minute or two, that's all."

"Yeah, I think we all need a little rest, especially him, the fat slob." The American indicated a prostrate Bormann who was lying on the ground, panting for breath like a stranded whale. "But not too long. The Popovs might just come back."

"I know. But this bank of the Havel is supposed to be held by German forces."

Bormann didn't understand English, but he did pick up the words "Havel" and "German" and guessed the rest. Of course, this was still German-held territory. With a bit of luck, he might just be able to escape from these two foreign crooks and appeal to the German military for help. After all he was dressed in the uniform of an SS major-general. Even in this eleventh hour, with Germany in chaos, the military still respected generals. Despite his exhaustion and the cold, Bormann started to feel a soft glow of hope spurt up inside him. He hadn't come this far and suffered so many dangers to allow himself to be handed over to the English tamely. No sir!

After they had rested five minutes, Kuehn got to his feet and pulled Bormann to his. "We're moving out," he said. The plan is to follow the course of the Havel till it runs into the Elbe. There we'll find the British."

Bormann said nothing. He simply stood there lamely as if his spirit had been broken completely.

"I reckon," van de Brug said to Kuehn, as he levered himself up, "it should take us two days or so to reach the British lines on the other side of the Elbe. I should imagine the German Army is in a process of disintegration, but there'll be some diehards, I don't doubt, who'll fight to the bitter end. If we run into any of those and they try to make trouble for us . . ." His hand dropped to his pistol, for they had left their machine pistols in the electric boat. "You know what to do?"

"I do," Kuehn said grimly. "Shoot first and ask questions afterwards." He gave Bormann a push. "All right, fatso, move it!"

Reluctantly, Bormann moved it . . .

It was a strange night, full of alarms and sudden frights. It was clear that this May night the Russians were making their final attack on the doomed capital. The thunder of the enemy barrage was now reaching its crescendo. Tracer zipped back and forth lethally. On all sides there was noise and sudden death.

Once they bumped into a tented German casualty clearing station. But the Russians had been there before them. Dead men lay on the stretchers outside. Inside, with the yellow lantern still hissing and sending out a blindlingly white light, there were empty bottles of surgical spirit and dead bodies of doctors and nurses everywhere. The nurses all had their knickers ripped down to their ankles and their white overalls, splattered with blood, thrown open. They had been raped. A dead surgeon, a great hole smashed in the back of his head, lay slumped over the man he had been operating on when the Russians had surprised them. His patient was dead, too, bayonets through the throat. Bormann was sick. Van de Brug and Kuehn calmly helped themselves to the flask of hot sweet tea, which the nurses had obviously used to pep the dead surgeon up.

Two hours later with the dirty white light of the false dawn flushing the sky to the east, they came to a rough cottage at the side of the water. Yellow light streamed from its shattered windows as if those inside had never heard of the blackout. Women were laughing and giggling drunkenly and from upstairs they could hear the rapid squeak of rusty bedsprings. "Christ," Kuehn said in awe, "at it like a Yiddish fidler's elbow!"

"Yes," van de Brug agreed, "let's leave the Casanovas to it, whoever they are. Come on." Silently, hardly daring to breathe, they crept by the lonely cottage, though Bormann would have dearly loved to have sounded the alarm just in case the "Casanovas" were German.

Another half an hour passed. They stumbled on, sticking to the shadows. More than once Bormann, his feet blistered, his chest heaving like an ancient cracked leathern bellows, threatened to fall out, but each time Kuehn tapped his pistol holster and rasped, "If you do, you're a dead man, Bormann." He kept going.

But now the real dawn was coming slowly, as if some god on high was reluctant to throw light on this terrible war-torn world below. Van de Brug stopped, licked his parched lips and said wearily, "We'd better get under cover for a while. We can rest and check the situation out before we go on."

"Agreed," Kuehn said, supporting a badly swaying Bormann with one hand. "He's had a noseful as it is."

Van de Brug suryeyed the war-torn landscape. Above Berlin, to their rear, there was a huge pall of black smoke, tinged with scarlet flame. To their front they could see the flashes of guns, but the firing was nothing like that over Berlin. Here, too, the terrain was empty, as if it had been abandoned or the soldiers had gone to ground, burying themselves deep under the earth. "See that weigh-master's cottage at one o'clock?"

Kuehn nodded. He had already seen several along the banks of the Havel. They were used by the authorities to check the weight of the barges which sailed the river to the Elbe, one of Europe's great waterways.

"Let's try that. Can't see anyone using it for military purposes."

"Right." Dragging Bormann who was virtually all-in, behind him, Kuehn followed the Dutchman, who advanced cautiously on the little house.

Van de Brug was taking no chances. Pistol in hand, crouched low, he circled the place, while Kuehn covered him. Cautiously he tried the door handle. It went down. With a rusty squeak, the door was opened. He sprang inside in one bound, pistol raised. But the place was empty and it was clear whoever had occupied it had made a hasty departure. There was a stale loaf of bread on the table with the breadsaw still stuck in it and a hunk of salami had been neatly cut on the wooden boards that the peasants used instead of plates. He flashed a hasty look around the interior. Nothing save that the picture of Hitler, which had once graced the wall, had been flung to the floor and the glass smashed.

. "All right, Al," he called softly. "The place's empty. They've done a bunk." He indicated the smashed photo of Hitler as a white knight riding a great stallion and carrying a swastika flag with a jerk of his pistol muzzle. "They obviously knew the dream was over. We'll be all right here for a while."

Bormann slumped down and closed his eyes.

# NINE

Bormann opened one eye carefully. It was midday and his two captors still snored lustily on the floor opposite him. They had taken away his boots and belt before they had lain down to sleep. But that didn't worry him. The track outside was earth. He'd find boots somewhere or other. The main thing was to escape while he still had a chance. For already he could hear the sound of gunfire. If it had woken him from an exhausted sleep, it might well waken them, too.

Slowly, very slowly, he rose and edged towards the door, holding up his breeches with his free hand. Hardly daring to breathe and praying that the door hinges wouldn't squeak, he turned the handle and began to open it. Behind him the two SS officers snored on happily, despite the increased noise of the gunfire. He licked suddenly parched lips and slid himself through the opening. He was out. He closed the door behind him and breathed out hard. He had escaped the kidnappers!

The keeper of the cottage had been growing beans before his flight. The young plants, now all dead from a lack of water, were attached to the canes by twine. Hastily he grabbed a few lengths and as he moved away, still on the tips of his toes, he tied them together to form a crude belt.

Now he had to make a decision. Should he stick to the

path or should he cross the fields to the little country road some two hundred metres away which ran parallel to the path? He decided on the road. There he was more likely to find military vehicles which would give him a lift, though at the moment the road seemed completely deserted.

He began to move swiftly across the fields, littered here and there with the dead, bloated carcasses of cows, their legs sticking rigidly in the air. He wrinkled his nose in disgust. The corpses stank to high heaven. The beasts must have been dead for days.

He burst through a hedge, looked left and right and saw the road was deserted save for a wrecked tank a couple of hundred metres away. A great gleaming silver hole had been skewered in the side of its turret and a dead tanker lay in the dust next to the shattered left track. A victim of an air attack, he told himself, and then steeling himself, he advanced on the wreck. With luck he might find the boots he needed, for the tarmac was hard and he could already feel his feet beginning to ache.

The dead man's stomach had been blown out by whatever projectile had struck the tank. Now his entrails lay in the dust at his side like a great monstrous snake. Bormann couldn't believe that a man's guts were that big. He swallowed hard and tried to fight off the bitter nausea that threatened to overcome him. He needed those boots. Trying to keep his lips shut tight so that he would not breathe in that awful stench of rotted flesh and shaking his head to ward off the great fat bluebottles which were everywhere feeding off that great gaping wound, he grunted and pulled off the dead man's first boot. The next one was more difficult. The soldier had fallen from the tank mortally wounded and had collapsed with one leg doubled beneath him. Now rigor mortis had set in and the leg was stiff and hard to bend.

Desperately, knowing that time was running out, he fought the hard stiff flesh, using all his weight, beads of dweat standing out on his narrow forehead like opaque pearls. Suddenly it gave. He heard a sharp click like a dry twig snapping underfoot in a dry summer and guessed he had broken the dead man's bone. Not that it mattered now. He was a stiff. What mattered, Bormann told himself as he pulled off the other boot, was that he, Martin Bormann continued to live. Hastily he tugged on the boots. They weren't a bad fit. They'd do him until he found some wheels. As an afterthought he tugged out the dead man's pistol from its holster and stuck it in his pocket. Finally he touched the side of his tunic. The diamonds and the money were still there. In their exhaustion his two captors, who, he knew, realised that he had some valuables on him, had forgotten to relieve him of them. He smiled and gave the dead man a mock salute, saying, "Thank you, soldier. The last head of the German National Socialist Party salutes you." Then he was gone, feeling very pleased with himself, heading westwards. He had done it, he told himself happily. He was on his way again . . .

Schulze mopped his brow with the ragged sleeve of his tunic. The noon sun was pretty hot for May and he had been forcing the pace, hoping that they were going in the right direction.

Next to him Matz, carrying Heidi's Schmeisser as well as his own, halted too. "Not a sign of the shits," he said and licked his parched lips. "God in heaven, what a heat. I'd give my left nut for a jar of ice-cold suds!"

Schulze sniffed. "Didn't think you had any nuts," he commented.

Now they could no longer hear the rumble of the

barrage descending on a doomed Berlin, but the rumble of gunfire to the West was getting ever louder and they knew they were slowly approaching the Elbe where they knew the British to be. It seemed, therefore, that the German defenders on the opposite bank were still putting up some kind of resistance.

Schulze and Matz swept their eyes over the flat sandy plain of the Elbe. To their right they could see a mushroom of smoke ascending to the bright blue, cloudless sky. Perhaps another victim of the dreaded *Jabos*, the enemy fighter-bombers, which were appearing in ever larger numbers now that the weather had turned perfect. Already twice this morning they had had to throw themselves wildly into the nearest ditch as a *Jabo* had come roaring in at tree-top heights, machine guns and cannon blazing furiously. Once, too, they had come across an ancient field-hand, dead in the middle of his ploughing, the back of his head blown off by a *Jabo*, with his horse still standing numbly between the shafts of the wrecked plough. "Horrible, just horrible," Heidi had cried, burying her worn face in her hands, "they're killing individual people," to which Corporal Matz had replied gently, "It's always been that way in war, Heidi. Old hares like me and Schulze get away with it time and time agen. It's the innocent what suffer most."

"All right," Schulze said, making up his mind, "we'd better take our hindlegs in our paws and start hoofing it agen. We're going in the right direction all right – westwards."

"Yes," Matz said, as the weary troopers rose to their feet and began shuffling down the country road that ran parallel to the Havel once more, "but we're heading right for the MFL" – he meant the main firing line – "as well."

211

"We'll worry about that problem when we come to it. Now cut the cackle and let's get on with it."

Half an hour, later they trailed silently through that wasted landscape. Now every crossroads seemed to have a shot-up tank, with bodies of its crew sprawled out grotesquely on the blood-stained cobbles. Once they filed wordlessly by a trek which had been attacked by the *Jabos*. The canvas-roofed wagons, with the stove pipes sticking through the covering, had been riddled with machine-gun fire. Horses lay slumped dead in the shafts and on both sides the fields were littered with the dead bodies of men, women and children who had been killed by the pursuing *Jabo* pilots. All seemed death and destruction, as if the enemy were determined to make Germany and the Germans suffer to the very bitter end.

It was about two that they spotted the column coming towards them. It was too far away for the suddenly alert Wotan troopers to make out who they were. But the persons advancing upon them slowly, dreadfully slowly, it seemed, gave off a stench that they could smell even at that distance. It was rancid and cloying, making them want to spit and choke. "Jesus," Schulze exclaimed, "it's like the stink at the monkey house at the zoo when my old man took me there as a kid. Who the shit can they be?"

Bormann, further up that road, asked himself that same question, as he stopped, uncertain of what to do next, peering at the weary column of what seemed mainly women, clad in the striped pyjama uniform of the concentration camps. Where were their guards? he asked himself. Rats like that should not be wandering around Germany's roads with no guards in sight. Suddenly he felt a righteous anger sweep through his plump body. He frowned and, thrusting out that pugnacious chin of his, he started walking once more.

Now he could see the skeletal wretches quite clearly. They advanced like grey boney ghosts, some of them dragging little carts heaped up with their pathetic little bits-and-pieces, faces hollowed out to death heads, eyes dull and listless under the striped caps. Some hobbled on sticks. One was being pushed by two others perched like some monstrous skeletal baby in a pram. And from them all came that throat-searing, nauseating odour that made him want to throw up.

He halted in the middle of the road, right in their path, legs astride, hands on his plump hips, every inch the German master race. *"Was geht denn hier vor?"* he demanded harshly, as the column faltered to a halt. "What's going on? Who are you? What are you rats up to?"

Nobody answered!

"Guards," he barked at the top of his voice. "Where in three devils' name are you?" He assumed the concentration camp guards, herding the column eastwards, would be to the rear.

Again no one answered.

Suddenly Bormann felt a twinge of fear. He was alone with perhaps two hundred or more of the wretches. Suddenly he was aware, too, that they were beginning to stare at the skull and crossbones insignia of their torturers on his cap. He swallowed hard. "Oh, well get on with it," he barked, trying to retain his composure. "Go to your deaths, you deserve it, rats like you."

The prisoners did not move, but now, to his alarm, Bormann could see their skeletal faces were beginning to be animated by some raw emotion. They were baring their teeth like animals, a dull red fury starting to blaze in their lacklustre eyes. Strange unintelligible sounds were coming from deep down in their skinny throats.

Hastily Bormann whipped out his looted pistol and whipped off the safety catch. "I'm warning you," he snarled with a trace of his old arrogance, "that I shall fire in one moment, if you don't move on. I shall count to three and then I'll shoot – er – *you*." He aimed the gun at a tall, skinny wretch with long lank grey hair, who might well have been a woman, though if she were she no longer possessed a figure.

Nobody moved.

Suddenly Bormann was overcome by a total unreasoning fear. He pressed the trigger. *Nothing happened!* He did so again, eyes abruptly wild with terror. *Nothing!* It had jammed. Or the magazine was empty. What was he to do? He staggered, eyes wide and wild with terror.

A low eerie keening started up from the mob of skeletons. It came from deep down inside them. For a few moments Bormann couldn't understand it. Then he caught the two single letters, "*S . . . S.*"

"*No!*" he shrieked, holding out his arms, hands upwards, as if to ward off the mob which had begun to shuffle towards him in a slow, terrifying, stiff-legged gaze, the ex-prisoners moving their legs with their hips, jerking from side to side. "*NO . . . NICHT SS!*" he screamed. "*NICHT SS!*"

Then they were on him, stick-like arms raining blow after blow upon him, chanting like some kind of litany. "*S . . . S . . . S . . . S . . .*" Screaming and shrieking for mercy, arms raised above his head in the classic pose of supplication, he went down. They started to kick him, many with bare, filthy feet. His nose broke. Blood gushed out of it in thick fury. The sight seemed to encourage their blind rage. Someone jabbed his heel in Bormann's right eye and started to gouge it out. Both cheeks burst.

His cheekbones glittered like polished ivory against the welter of red gore. By now he had stopped screaming. He simply lay there and let it happen. Then he was dead and they stopped . . .

# TEN

The survivors of Wotan stared down in awed silence at the remains of the once most powerful man in the Third Reich after Hitler. The concentration camp ex-inmates had literally trampled him to pulp before they had started trudging eastwards once again, past the ditch where they had hidden themselves till they had gone. Probably every bone in Bormann's fat body was broken. Now he lay squashed to the cobbles in a welter of scarlet gore, face pressed deep into the stone.

Heidi stared down at him with the rest. She could feel no sympathy for her former boss. He had died, like he had lived, in a rough, brutal fashion – just an animal.

Schulze felt no compassion either. He said, "That's the way they should all die. They sent off young German lads to die on fronts over three Continents. But they never had any shit flung at them. They hoped to die nice and peaceful in bed. This sod didn't. But the rest probably will." He sighed a little wearily and said, "Come on, lads. It's about time we got moving agen."

"Hey, wait a mo," Matz objected.

Schulze swung round on him. "Did you open your sausage-swallower, arse-with-ears?"

"I did," Matz answered promptly. "What about the frigging loot?"

"Oh that. Holy strawsack, I'd forgotten all about

the loot." He stopped and looked back at Bormann's squashed body.

Next to him, Heidi wrung her hands and said, "Oh, don't, Sergeant Schulze. It's unclean. You don't want anything from that monster or all the others like him. They're finished. They're part of history. It's blood money after all." She clutched his big paw, as if physically attempting to restrain him.

He laughed easily. "*Fraulein*," he said, "money don't stink, as the old saying goes. We've got to eat." He looked at Matz. "Corporal Matz, you search him."

"What?"

"You heard, plush ears."

Wringling his nose in distaste, Matz bent and turned the crumpled body of the Party boss over. His shattered hands lolled to his sides like paper. Matz swallowed hard and forced himself to open the blood-soaked tunic and feel it. "There's something here," he said thickly.

Heidi turned away, but Schulze was unmoved. "Well, frigging well find out what it is," he ordered.

Almost delicately, Matz fished inside the tunic and brought out a thick bundle of bloodstained notes. "Money," he said and tossed them to Schulze.

Schulze caught the bundle easily in his big paw and whistled softly. "Dollars – American dollars. Hundreds of them, lads." He raised his voice. "Lads, for once we're not up to our hooters in shit. It's what's left of Wotan's lucky day . . ."

"Not really," a quiet, but confident voice said behind them.

Schulze spun round. Van de Brug and Kuehn stood there, pointing their pistols at the handful of Wotan troopers. Kuehn jerked up the muzzle of his weapon and snapped harshly. "All right, you bunch of sows, drop your weapons. *Los, wird's bald?*"

Slowly, very slowly, the Wotan troopers started to unbuckle their weapons.

"Move it," Kuehn urged, eyes glinting dangerously, "or somebody's going to get hurt *soon!*"

One by one the weapons clattered to the cobbles, while the troopers stared at the two officers, on their hard, worn faces a mixture of frustration and defiance. Van de Brug moved forward and not lowering his pistol for a moment kicked the weapons into the ditch that ran along the side of the road. Then he turned his attention to Matz, still crouched over the dead body of Bormann. "See what else you can find in the lucky dip. Go on." Again he jerked up the muzzle of his pistol threateningly.

Reluctantly Matz started to search further in that blood-soaked tunic, feeling the broken ribcage creaked unpleasantly under his touch.

Meanwhile Kuehn had turned to Schulze and barked, "All right, you big bastard, give me the money. And no funny tricks. Got it?"

Schulze moved forward as if to give the money to the one-armed van de Brug. Kuehn halted him in his tracks. "Not to the *Hauptsturm,*" he warned. "To me – and throw it."

Inwardly Schulze cursed. He had thought the one-armed van de Brug might have lowered his pistol to take the money, then he would have rushed him. But that wasn't to be. Miserably he tossed the grinning American the bundle of bloodstained dollar bills. Kuehn's grin broadened as he tucked them safely inside his own tunic with fingers that had abruptly turned red.

At the body, Matz found the little leather bag of gems. He opened the drawstring. The diamonds glittered and

218

sparkled. "Christ," he told himself, "they must be worth a frigging king's ransom."

"That's them," van de Brug said smartly, knowing that it had to be the bag that Kuehn had felt through the cloth of the tunic that day. "Now, put them on the ground and, easy does it, kick them over to me. *Verstehen*?"

"*Verstehen*," Matz answered sullenly.

He dropped the bag of precious stones to the cobbles and then with the toe of his boot, he kicked the bag towards van de Brug. The latter bent, still keeping his pistol levelled and picked it up. "Well," he said, "we've lost part of our ticket to freedom." He indicated the squashed body of the *Reichsleiter*. "But these will, undoubtedly, make up for that loss."

"Cut the crap," Schulze snapped harshly. "What are you going to do with us?"

Van de Brug returned his hard, challenging look. "What do you think, you big-horned ox." He raised his pistol.

The *Jabo* came hurtling across the flat Elbe plain at 400 mph, machine guns and cannon chattering already. In an instant 20mm cannon shells glowing white and lethal were exploding all around them. Van de Brug screamed, shrill and hysterical like a woman, as a cannon shell shattered his wooden arm and exploded at his side. The impact threw him a couple of metres to one side of the road. He was dying already even before he slumped into the ditch, diamonds from the burst bag showering everywhere over his dying body.

"*Take cover*," Schulze bellowed and, grabbing a startled Heidi's hand, flung her into the ditch in the same moment that Kuehn fired and missed.

The *Jabo*, a gleaming silver in the rays of the sun, howled round in a tight turn, leaving a thin brown trail behind it, before straightening out once more. Now it came zooming right down the dead-straight road at tree-top height, cannon chattering frantically, 20mm shells slammed into the cobbles. Furious angry-red sparks erupted in a long deadly line. Two Wotan troopers lying flat in the road were hit. Their bodies rose, arched spines like taut bows, faces contorted with unbearable pain and agony. A third was hit in mid-stride as he ran for the cover of the ditch. His hands clawed the air, as if he were climbing the rungs of an invisible ladder. Desperately he tried to keep upright. To no avail. As the fighter-bomber flashed by them, its prop wash whipping and lashing their uniforms about their skinny bodies, the Wotan trooper slammed to the cobbles, dead.

*"Fuck it all, you dumb American bastard!"* Al Kuehn cried in English shaking his fist at the plane, carried away by an almost unbearable fury. He ran to where van de Brug's shattered body lay. Frantically he started to grab the gems from it with his free hand, cursing and muttering to himself like a man demented, eyes wide, wild and crazy.

Then he was up and running down the road, stuffing the gems into his pockets, shrieking at the American plane and its pilot, while behind him the Wotan troopers safe in the ditch yelled, "Get down, you crazy shit! Get down!"

But Al Kuehn wasn't listening. He'd survive, he always had. He'd survived North Africa, Sicily, D-Day, when every other man of his company in the "Big Red One" had been cut down on Omaha Beach. No one, but no one was going to kill him now.

Again the American Thunderbolt did a tight turn. This time the pilot lowered his undercarriage and flaps to slow the fighter-bomber down to almost stalling speed. This time he was determined he'd finish off the Krauts below. That morning the CO had told the crews in the briefing room that a ceasefire with the Germans would come into force at sixteen hundred hours this day. Now this would be his last chance ever to kill Krauts – and he wasn't going to miss it. He placed his thumb on the teat of the bomb toggle, eyes taking in the sole Kraut running down the centre of the little country road below, as if he had gone crazy. "Bomb happy," he said to himself through gritted teeth. He'd use the guy who'd gone apeshit as his aiming point.

Now he'd have to be careful. He was very low and very slow. He didn't want to explode the bomb directly under his plane. That might mean curtains for him. He caught the white blur of the running man's face beneath the silver belly of the Thunderbolt. He seemed to be shouting. "Silly S.O.B.," he told himself and pressed the teat.

The Thunderbolt lurched as the 250 pound bomb dropped from the fuselage. The pilot caught the controls just in time. He pressed back the throttle to increase his speed and then he was winging away to the west, as the bomb screeched to its target.

"*Volle Deckung* . . . hit the dirt!" Schulze yelled urgently as the bomb hurtled out the sky. He pressed his face to the earth, mouth gaping open like that of some village idiot so that the blast wouldn't burst his eardrums.

Suddenly the ground heaved and trembled like a live thing. Earth showered down on his helmet. Hot blast rushed past him. For a moment he was too dazed to look up. Then he shook his head like a man trying to waken from a deep sleep. He blinked his eyes. Everything came back into focus as he raised his head to peer over the side of the ditch.

A great steaming black-charred hole had suddenly

appeared in the centre of the road about a hundred metres away. "Anyone hurt?" Schulze called, hardly recognizing his own voice.

"No," a succession of shocked, relieved voices answered.

Schulze got to his feet warily and scanned the May sky. But it was empty. The *Jabo* had vanished, its job done. Slowly he pulled himself out of the ditch, picking up a Schmeisser as he did so. Carefully, the machine pistol clutched to his side, finger tensed on the trigger, he advanced on the hole, searching the ditch on either side for the first sight of the American. But both sides were empty. Then he saw why.

Lying in the road, just behind the great steaming hole, lay a single severed hand, still clutching a pistol. It was that of Lieutenant Kuehn.

Matz came limping up, together with Heidi. "Where's the *Ami* swine?" he demanded.

Wordlessly, Schulze pointed to the lone hand in the road.

Heidi gave a little moan and turned her head away quickly.

Matz said, "And where's the rest of him?"

Schulze shrugged. "Gone up the spout, I suppose. That bomb must have shredded him like a butcher's grinder."

"And the money . . . the diamonds?" Matz asked almost angrily. "What happened to the loot?"

Again Schulze shrugged. "*Gone!*" he answered laconically. "*All shitting gone!*" Suddenly he started to laugh, low at the start, then rising and rising till it became a full-scale roar.

"What's there to laugh about?" Matz began almost angrily and then he was laughing, too.

222

Thus they stood there on the little country road in the warm May sunshine, a handful of "old hares", weary, unshaven, hungry, with nothing in the world but the rags they stood up in, roaring with laughter as if they had just heard the funniest joke in the world; while Hcidi watched them, shaking her pretty young head and whispering to herself, "Mad . . . all men are mad . . . *MAD* . . ."

# ENVOI

"War is hell, but peacetime'll kill you."

*The Sayings of Sergeant Schulze*

Slowly, but steadily, the two soldiers and the girl advanced on the outskirts of the Harz township of Goslar. There they would leave her in the hope Heidi would find some kind of transport to take her home to her parents. The other Wotan troopers had already broken up in different directions after dumping their weapons in the River Elbe.

Already it seemed the war had been over for a long time. The Sherman tank they were passing was already beginning to rust; and the 88mm gun which had knocked it out before the crew had abandoned it was already beginning to disappear in the lush grass and the new spring flowers. A strange stillness lay over the countryside, which they had to keep telling themselves was not strange. It was just that the continuous barrage had ceased.

Here and there to left and right, aged farm workers were out, clearing their fields of the debris of war. Shell holes were being filled. Abandoned weapons were being dragged away by teams of great lumbering red and white oxen. It was as if man and nature were together attempting to hide the fact that there had ever been a war. When the workers looked and spotted the two men in *Wehrmacht* uniform, they stared at them in a puzzled manner, as if wondering who these strange creatures could be. German soldiers? But Germany had lost the war. What were they doing, still wandering about in the uniform of the defeated army? Then they bent their heads again to their tasks and dismissed the soldiers from their thoughts.

"What are you going to do, Sergeant Schulze and Corporal Matz?" Heidi asked. Now she was dressed in a rough tweed skirt and a pullover over her soldier's shirt which they had found in a ruined house.

They paused at the bullet-pocked metal sign announcing they had reached the outskirts of Goslar.

Schulze shoved his cap to the back of his cropped head. "First thing, I'd say, is to get rid of this uniform. We ain't got no discharge papers and the Tommies could pick us up and put us behind the wire at any time."

Matz nodded his approval vigorously. "No buck-toothed Tommy is gonna put me in the cage. So, *Fraulein* Heidi, we've got to get civvies." He paused momentarily and looked down at the shabby, dirty field grey uniform with the eagle-and-swastika badge torn off the breast, as if seeing it for the very first time. "Be funny though," he continued, "haven't worn civvies since 1939."

Schulze tugged at the end of his big nose, red from the May sun. "It'll be funny though, I agree, Matzi. We've had our fun in this war, haven't we? The gash, the suds, the larks with the other lads, and all the rest of it." He frowned hard, as if he were finding it difficult to express himself correctly. "But we paid the price, didn't we, in blood and misery? Life was so frigging cheap. Remember old Sergeant Dietz back in '43 just before the Battle of Kursk?"

Matz nodded, while the girl looked up at the big man, his face somehow wretched as he attempted to put his thoughts into words.

"He said I could have his new leather jacket if he got

the chop. Well, he did and what was the first thing I did when they hauled the body out of his tank? I'll tell yer. I said, 'Hey watch that frigging jacket o' mine!' Heartless we were, all of us. Frigging heartless."

Instinctively Heidi reached out and pressed his great horny paw. "You could never be heartless, Sergeant Schulze," she assured him winningly. "I . . ."

She stopped short. A British jeep was cruising slowly down the road. In front there sat two soldiers in peaked redcaps. "Military police," Schulze said, voice normal again. "Fraulein Heidi, I think it's about time we did a bunk."

Matz said, "And here, *Fraulein*, here's something for you. Help you along a bit when you get home." He thrust something hard, wrapped in a dirty handkerchief into her hand. Then both had turned and were walking quickly in the other direction to the jeep.

Slowly the British jeep cruised by the lone girl, standing there a little forlornly. The two MPs gave Heidi a hard searching look in the manner of their kind, then apparently satisfied, they turned and went back the way they had come.

Heidi remembered the gift, or whatever it was, and Matz's words, "help you along a bit". She unwrapped the dirty cloth and gasped. It was one of Bormann's gems. Her eyes filled with tears. Here they were, on the run, members of a criminal organisation, the SS, and they had given her the only thing of value they possessed. She dabbed her eyes. Slowly she started up the street to the centre of Goslar. "I'll never forget you," she whispered to herself. But, of course, she would. Time, age, the worries of family life would, over the years, make that moment fade and fade until she would wonder if it had not all been a dream . . .

Schulze and Matz came out of their hiding place and watched the jeep drive away to be followed by the girl's slow progress uphill. Schulze took the last "flatman" from his tattered tunic, pulled out the plug and took a tremendous slug of the firewater, his Adam's apple going up and down his throat like an express lift. He belched and handed what was to left to an envious Matz, already licking his lips in anticipation. "Here, old house," he said jovially, "whip that down behind your collar-stud." Which Matz promptly did.

"Now," Schulze said, eyes sparkling suddenly, "where to now, Matzi?"

Matz finished off the schnapps and threw the bottle away carelessly. After all it was yet another "dead soldier", one of the thousands the two of them must have consumed in the last six years of war. "Who the fuck cares, Schulzi?" he cried challengingly. "We've been up to our hooters in shit before. Many a time. And we're still here, aren't we?"

"Of course, we are, my little piece of apeturd," Schulze cried back enthusiastically. He gave the little man a great slap across the back that sent him staggering forward, his wooden leg creaking in protest. "What have we allus said, Matzi – march or croak. *So let's frigging well march!*" Arm in arm the two old comrades set off up the long winding white road that led into the Harz mountains, singing lustily one of their old SS marching songs, as if they hadn't a care in the world . . .